ANGELA JACKSON was recently named one of Edinburgh UNESCO City of Literature's emerging writers. By day, she is a coach and a lecturer in psychology and education. She has written features for various newspapers including the *Guardian* and the *Independent*. *The Emergence of Judy Taylor* is her first novel.

THE EMERGENCE OF JUDY TAYLOR

ANGELA JACKSON

Constable & Robinson Ltd
55–56 Russell Square
London WC1B 4HP
www.constablerobinson.com

First published in the UK by Canvas,
an imprint of Constable & Robinson Ltd., 2013

Published in this paperback edition by Canvas, 2013

Angie Durbin has kindly given permission to use her font,
Angelina, on page 65.

This is a work of fiction. Names, characters, places and incidents are either
the product of the author's imagination or are used fictitiously.

A copy of the British Library Cataloguing in
Publication data is available from the British Library.

ISBN 978-1-47210-165-5 (paperback)
ISBN 978-1-47210-497-7 (ebook)

Printed and bound by CPI Group (UK) Ltd, Croydon, CR0 4YY

3 5 7 9 10 8 6 4 2

This book is dedicated to David, Tom, Grace and Joe,
with all my love and heartfelt gratitude

WHEN MATHEMATICIANS LOOK AT crowd behaviour, they see beautiful fractal patterns. In their eyes, we swoop and soar like a murmuration of starlings, all as one. Those who break away from the flock, in pursuit of anomie, go on to create the same recurring shapes elsewhere. Our brains, our lungs and the miles of arteries, veins and capillaries within each of us mirror the natural forms of trees, seashells and tributaries. Even our differences unite us. The beating hearts of Olympic runners and trading-floor bankers, of paediatric surgeons and the innocent under oath are saved by minute irregularities imperceptible to the human ear. Mathematicians know that we are all dancing to the same tune, whatever, whoever and wherever we are.

CHAPTER 1

IT WAS THE TYPE of wedding that drew people in like a cyclone, picking them up at various points, stilling them in the rarefied zone of the eye and spewing them out again when it was all over. It was the type of wedding where decisions over stationery had been taken slowly, after turning heavy pages of samples and listening to a woman with a geography degree offer her thoughts on crisp white, pure ivory and duck-egg-blue stock. A wedding where guests had been given the opportunity to choose the perfect gift from a list sorted by ascending price on a department store's website, have it gift-wrapped, labelled 'With all our love and best wishes for the future' or 'To a lovely couple' and sent to an address of the bride and groom's choosing or held until they returned from honeymoon.

It was a wedding with pews full of guests dressed in pastels and navy or charcoal, the women understated so as not to upstage the bride on her special day. A wedding with ushers who knew where to seat people without asking. A wedding with a bride who rebelled with cream satin; no white meringue for her. A wedding with a best man who would pat his pocket blankly, then laugh as he pulled out the rings. A wedding with a mother of the bride in pink chiffon, a father of the groom two malts down, noisy children, a left-wing deaf aunt, a right-wing, cantankerous old uncle with plenty of fight left in him.

It was a wedding with a bitter photographer who had once fancied himself as the next David Bailey. A wedding with a vicar who had christened the groom and, two years later, the bride, and had seen them every Christmas morning and Easter Sunday since. A vicar who knew them by sight, by reputation, by the blood that coursed through their veins. He would christen their children and bury their parents, offering guarantees from a higher power that may or may not exist.

Waiters and waitresses streamed out of the kitchen like ants, holding silver trays of prawn cocktail and green salad. There was a bit of fumbling over cutlery but not much, and nobody minded. Mums warmed foil-wrapped butter in their palms for the children, and buttered bread sparingly for those wearing dry-clean-only clothes. The lamb was a bit undercooked for some. The vegetarians had no complaints about their customary goat's cheese filo parcels. The dessert contained flower petals and had been created to resemble a shower of confetti, but such artistry was lost on all but the kitchen staff. Despite evidence to the contrary, in the form of most petals returning untouched, the chef was reassured that the meal had been a resounding success. It was a wedding like any other.

The speeches contained only the kindest words for the beautiful bride and her lovely maids. Each sentence had been carefully calibrated to present the groom as worldly but loyal, naughty but nice. There were hints of schtum being kept. A nose was tapped, a wink given. Say no more. The best jokes came from the best man. The father of the bride had been duly warned by the mother of the bride moments before he rose to his feet: don't sing; nobody wants to hear you sing. And we've heard all your jokes, thank you. Stick to the facts and sit down. He received a patted knee and a tight smile for his compliance.

The groom twirled his prize to Paul Weller and the click and flash of every camera in the room. Children stood on their grandparents' feet and pretended to waltz. Uncles remembered when Elvis was king and pulled at quiffs long gone. Someone did an impression of Bez. Everyone danced to Abba with their arms in the air because it was the law.

The chief bridesmaid caught the bouquet, of course. The florist wire scratched her but she didn't flinch. She held aloft the pale roses and peonies, like Liberty holds her torch, and welcomed all comers: the tired, the hungry, the tempest-tossed, the best man at a push.

Judy had married Oliver and discarded her surname without a second thought. She had promised to love and honour him, and he had promised to do all kinds of things until death parted them. They had drunk too much champagne to consummate their marriage in the frills and flounces of the honeymoon suite, but put things right in Hawaii, once they'd got over the jet lag. They returned two weeks later, skidding down in Manchester rain, tanned and happy, suitcases bulging with spirits and perfume.

Some years passed.

CHAPTER 2

J UDY SAT IN HER kitchen, on her favourite dining chair, and
surveyed the chipped navy blue polish on her toenails. She
wasn't exactly avoiding going back into the living room – she
would have to go back in at some point – but her face was
aching a little from responding to the long-awaited news that
her brother and his partner were expecting a baby. It had been
a genuine smile at first, of course, but the details – and there
were many – had required a sustained positive facial response,
and because she had started at such a broad grin, she had felt
backed into a corner. At one point, she had managed to
shoehorn in an expression of surprise – a perfect O with her
mouth (the relief!) – but, foolishly, foolishly, she'd segued from
that to a laugh and, damn it, back to a rictus grin.

So, she felt she deserved to linger a little over the coffee-
making duties. She reflected that she had spent many months
organizing her features into various appropriate responses to

the barrage of information relating to the vagaries of trying for a baby.

The top notes of Alicia Keys drifted across the hall, and the low rumble of men speaking was punctuated by an occasional girly laugh. The kitchen radio chatted at a barely audible level about bees and climate change.

'Ooh, something smells good in here! Is it my wife?'

'It's the coffee.'

'Is everything all right?' Oliver hunched down and placed his hands on Judy's lap for stability.

'I'm tired,' she whispered.

'Me, too, but the coffee will perk you up. Come on!' He jumped up to finish making it. Judy knew by the way he opened a bag of Amaretto biscuits with his teeth that she wouldn't be sleeping any time soon.

He bounced back to their guests, sploshing coffee about as though they didn't have a cream carpet. Once upon a time, before the carpet, Judy had liked him wine-fuelled. Now, her irritation was so closely correlated with each glass he consumed that she had all but erased those purple memories.

'Min, tell Jude what the doctor said about a C-section …'

Already, blood from her brother.

Min picked up where Rob had left off: 'She said that if that's what I want, she'll put it in my notes and that someone would talk to me about it closer to the time …'

'But, obviously, we want the peace of mind *now* that we can have a C-section. If Min gets stressed, her blood pressure could go up and then there's the risk of —'

'Rob, what do you mean by "we"? *You*'re not going to be having a C-section, are you?' Judy popped Rob's bubble in the special way only siblings could.

'Whatever Min goes through, I'll be going through.' He was slurring slightly now, and petulant. He'd always been good at petulant.

'Course you will, mate,' said Oliver. 'It stands to reason after all you've been through.'

'She also said that I'll have to be careful around raw egg, and obviously I use raw eggs all the time.' Min was a chocolatier. She poured so much into those moulds that there seemed little of her left after the working day. Her chocolate bars and truffles were flavoured with violet, cardamom, myrrh, sea salt – she'd once done a Manchester-tart truffle for a soap star's birthday party, but had declined the opportunity to create a Lancashire hot-pot confection.

'I wondered if you fancied a little part-time job, Jude,' ventured Min, nervously.

'Doing what?' asked Judy, her hackles now on overtime.

'Well, all the egg-based stuff at least. And anything that smells strong. I'm getting a bit sensitive.'

'Clearly not,' said Judy.

'Sorry?'

'Min, I have a job. I'm a lecturer. I teach. I teach music.'

'Only part-time! You're hardly ever there! And it's the summer holidays!' piped up Rob.

'Well, she does spend a lot of time working from home, preparing lessons and stuff, don't you, darling? And then

7

there's the private students she sees here.' Oliver stroked his wife's knee.

'Min, I'm sorry. I don't want to upset you, but I don't want or need a "little part-time job", if it's all the same to you.'

'I just thought I'd offer, that's all.'

Rob pulled Min closer. 'There's no need to take offence, Jude. It was my idea, anyway. I thought you'd be up for it.'

'Well, I'm not.'

It had been a long day, and the evening broke up a few minutes later. Among the hugs and gentle back-slapping, there were murmurings of 'No harm done', 'No offence taken' and 'Look after yourself', as the front door let in a blast of blissfully cool fresh air.

Oliver realized that any chance of having sex tonight was now thoroughly scuppered. He'd been working up to it all evening: a shower, a shave, his Calvin Klein boxers, drinking just enough but not too much, playing the right music, helping with the coffee, telling his best stories and winking at Judy as Rob and Min laughed at his punchlines. He'd lined it up like a World Cup penalty and here he was running up to a burst ball.

'Seriously, if I hear any more about this baby, I won't be responsible for my actions. We've got another six months of it, you know. And as for the fucking egg whites!' Judy shoved cups and plates into the dishwasher as Oliver blew out candles.

'I know! What a nerve! As if you'd say yes!'

'Is that what she thinks? Does she think my job's so pointless that I can drop it to go across town to whisk egg whites and shield her from the smell of bloody cocoa beans?'

'I know. She really has a nerve!' He kissed the back of her neck as he plopped a wooden spoon into the sink.

'I didn't spend four years at university so I could whisk egg whites!'

He slid his hands around her waist. Ever hopeful. Ever the optimist. 'Perhaps we should go up and practise some baby-making of our own.' He nuzzled her neck.

'Not tonight, Ol.'

CHAPTER 3

JUDY WAS GIVEN A Tiny Tears for her third birthday. From the day she tugged it out of its box, she became almost permanently attached to the doll, and remained so throughout the cold and wet summer of 1980, lisping her secrets and dreams into its ear, cradling, feeding, stroking it, dragging it by one arm to the dining-table, tucking it in with her at night. She changed its nappy and smeared its face with her mum's lipstick and eye shadow. The doll was the only one who listened when Judy said that she really hated carrots and that she wanted to stay all day at the play park, yes, until it was dark. It was always on Judy's side in any argument with stupid Robert, and kept her company when she was sulking. It was her sister, her baby, her constant companion. It was her solace when Robert and his naughty friends would stamp on her sandcastles or put woodlice in her dolls' house. It would cry when Judy cried.

Years later, when Tiny Tears was long forgotten, Judy would take gaggles of bright and beautiful friends home for tea. They would jostle around the kitchen table, listening to the radio, painting their fingernails with glittery polish, discussing the merits of Mark over Robbie, Jason, Howard and Gary. And when her brother barged in with his loud and hairy friends, she would hug her knees to her chin and watch over her scrapes and scars, appalled, as her friends swallowed their clever words, as they sweetened and quietened and blinked like baby deer. Later, she would tell them about Rob's filthy bedroom and his friends' terrible table manners, and they would listen agog as their crushes were made real by their flaws. Weekend by weekend, the boys would loiter longer in the kitchen, until one Saturday night when they chose to play an inevitable game of spin the bottle, and kissed their future wives under flickering fluorescent tubes.

Eventually, unexpectedly, Judy came to like Rob. He was no longer fascinated by woodlice and his friends were certainly improving as each year passed. He also had his uses: she was allowed to stay out later if Mum and Dad knew her big brother was with her, and he was the first in their circle of friends to buy a car, which meant she was ferried about quite a bit. It wasn't the blossoming of a deep friendship exactly, and hugs were strictly for Christmas and birthdays, but they found they could occupy adjacent spaces quite comfortably. They could take turns speaking without arguing, although neither felt they wanted to confide in the other, despite an absolute and implicit trust between them. In truth, their relationship worked best in the company of other people, who seemed to function rather like a couple of alcohol units, making things easier, looser.

Oliver Worthing came from the more verdant side of town, a bus ride away, where houses had driveways and double front doors, where one had to stroll rather than reach to knock on a neighbour's door. His mother was a part-time university lecturer and his father a senior partner at a local law firm; they paid people to mow their grass and clean under the lavatory rim. They read books and played bridge and bought tickets for the ballet, which they would later pass on to friends at short notice because of an impending migraine or late meeting. They had hoped their only child would spread his wings further afield than the university literally around the corner, but most of his friends were headed there, and that was all he had seemed interested in at the time. When he had first taken Judy home, they had attempted to mask their reservations with good manners. They didn't exactly bring out the best china, but tea was always poured from a pot for her, and when the guest room was eventually redecorated, the new curtains and bedlinen were in Judy's favourite colour (although Judy suspected that this was their way of telling her she would never sleep in their son's bedroom).

Over the years, the Worthings had come to almost love her, especially when she played the piano at their parties. On a final sustained chord, they would drape a proprietorial arm across her shoulders or kiss her lightly on the head before turning to their applauding friends with the delusional smiles of misplaced pride. What they really loved was that their son was happy. And he was. Oliver was very happy.

CHAPTER 4

'AND THE GOVERNMENT SPENDING cuts mean that we also have to look at not only our intake but our retention figures, too. I know we managed to get the figure down last year, but I think we could shave another 1 per cent off it, which would mean that our retention rate would be half a per cent lower than St George's and roughly in line with Xavier's although, as we all know, their published figures might not be telling us the whole story. Obviously, there's a lot of work to be done either way and, to that end, Martha has prepared a presentation on how we might go about supporting our students to stay the course – or should that be stay *on* the course? Ha! Martha?'

Martha Jones smiled at the principal and headed towards the front of the lecture theatre, pen drive first. After much fumbling and general IT incompetence, a thirty-one-page PowerPoint loaded on to the Smartboard. The first page simply read:

MARTHA JONES, BA, MIC

Head of Student Services

Student Retention: A Key Issue For Us **All**

This was going to be a long one.

'Have you got any mints?'

'What?'

'Mints. Have you got any? My mouth's really scuzzy after talking all day.'

Judy fumbled in her bag for mints for Paul Roberts.

'Does my breath smell?' He breathed audibly into her face. Martha Jones, BA, MIC, spotted it and gave him the teacher's eye. She'd obviously picked that up somewhere.

'Shut up. Here!' Judy handed him a roll of mints.

'Why? Are you that interested in learning how we're supposed to keep the students we're all trying to get rid of? Do you really want to keep the likes of Jemma Pitt all year?'

They both smirked and crunched mints over Martha's interminable presentation.

Paul had known Judy since they were children. They'd finally become friends at university, and had seen each other through the usual crises and celebrations since. He'd been Judy and Oliver's best man, and their wedding guests were still using his jokes years later. He was the most talented art tutor the college had, but had been twice passed over for the head of department post. His colleagues teased that it was because everyone knew his heart was in football rather than in art. However, it didn't help that his partner was a bit too high-profile with her drugs for the college's liking. Jen had almost single-handedly kept her dealer solvent since the Hacienda closed down, and was, at this very moment, giving a cocaine-fuelled blow job to someone who swore he used to dance in the clubs with Jason Orange.

Several decades later, slide thirty-one made its welcome appearance. 'Any questions? Comments?' Martha seemed blissfully unaware that she had sucked the life out of the room and had caused more than a couple of staff to consider risking the wrath of the principal by walking out before the slides had hit double figures. In the absence of questions, Martha checked her watch and saw that she had, by rights, another five minutes on the stage, so she puffed out her chest and launched into what she considered a motivational recap. It was too much for two members of staff, and they left the room by running out doubled over, as if they were trying to preserve everyone's view of Martha's final page:

RETENTION
A KEY ISSUE FOR US **ALL**
WHAT WILL YOU DO?

'I think retention is a key issue for Martha,' whispered Paul. 'Check out those ankles.'

'Don't be mean.'

'I've just sat through thirty PowerPoint pages. I *feel* mean.'

'Thirty-one.'

'Thirty-one PowerPoint pages. Now I feel even meaner.'

'I don't see how we can retain students who don't want to be here,' said Judy. 'It makes our job a bloody nightmare. What are we going to do? Lock them in cages? We're already paying them to turn up!'

'Judy?' Martha wanted her to share what she was saying with everyone else.

'I was just saying that you raised some important points, Martha. I have nothing to add.'

The teacher's eye again.

'OK. In that case, thank you. There are copies of this presentation on the intranet,' the sound of bags, files and coats being collected now drowned her voice, 'and I've produced some printed handouts you can pick up on the way out. There will be audio copies for anyone who would prefer them to printed versions, and anyone who wishes the presentation to be produced for them in another format or would like it translated, please let me know and I'll arrange for that to be done. Thank you.' She smiled at everyone's back as though they had been an adoring audience.

The principal started to clap and turned to the assembled staff to join in. Martha felt a warm glow and basked in the half-hearted applause, oblivious that they were really clapping the prospect of home.

CHAPTER 5

'HOLD STILL.'
THE NEEDLE pierced the skin just below Judy's right nipple, bringing tears to her eyes as a nurse drew fluid from her breast.

'Well done, Judy. Now, just hold this pad in place for a moment.' Judy wondered why nurses congratulated their patients on the ability to do nothing. She wanted to ask what would happen next but was still too shocked to form actual words, so she focused on pressing the gauze square against her flesh.

The nurse bustled around, then made some notes before turning back to Judy. 'We'll have the results for you later today, so can I ask you to come back at four o'clock?'

Decades passed in those few hours.

When Judy returned to the calming, pastel-walled waiting room, she held her book and made a reading face. The words pooled and whirled into nothing readable. She thought of Oliver. He'd been so insistent about coming with her. She'd wanted to be alone, but now she realized that she'd made a mistake. She took a mental snapshot of people who knew she was there. She imagined Oliver at his desk, probably frowning. Then the screen split and there was Gina, jabbing at her iPad, scaring herself silly on Google Images with flow charts and cheap wigs. And then she thought of Rob at work, watching the clock; she saw Paul encouraging his students to let go of their inner critic and paint; Mum cleaning, looking at the phone, cleaning again; Dad, probably watching *Countdown*, enjoying his retirement.

'Judith Worthing?'

Judy jumped at the sound of her name. The auxiliary gave her a reassuring smile, ushered her into an empty office and disappeared.

1980: the Clarks lady pressing on her toes to see if her new shoes were the right size.
1981: dancing around the living room in a pink leotard and tutu, watching a princess marry a prince.
1995: kissing Oliver until their mouths tasted of four a.m.
2000: the smell of fireworks. Veuve Clicquot. An engagement ring.
2001: confetti and smiles everywhere.
2012: a lump just under the right nipple.

A smiling nurse swept in. 'Judy?'

'Yes.'

Hello. I'm a nurse, whose name you'll not hear, but whose face you'll study harder than your future child's, checking for tells, for signs of strain or discomfort. I'm going to let you know where you go from here. I have the golden ticket, the black cap, the Tardis and St Peter's list.

'… and it was completely normal … hormones … cyclical breast pain … a well-fitting bra … a healthy diet.' She talked and talked, and the words just fell into the gap between the two women. Judy made a convincing listening face and the young junior nurse gave her patient all the information she thought she needed. Judy accepted a leaflet, said, 'Thank you,' and emerged from the hospital into a rainstorm that cleared the streets of pramming mothers and truanting teenagers in seconds.

The howling wind blew Judy's umbrella inside out for the third time. The number seven bus sailed past, drenching her right foot. It stopped a few metres ahead, and she ran to catch it. Too slow. It pulled away in a roar of black exhaust fumes. Had she been a bit quicker, she'd be sitting on that bus now, gently steaming through narrow streets of terraced houses towards a hot cup of tea and a change of clothes. She squelched slowly to the bus shelter. Completely normal. The phrase whirled around her head. Absolutely 100 per cent normal. Nothing going on. No shadows, nothing.

The waitress placed a second hot chocolate (with cream, this time) in front of Judy. The number twenty-threes rolled by the window every twelve minutes. Every one that stopped and left without her made her feel closer to something else.

At 17.01, she said goodbye to her mum and dad's dutiful daughter.

At 17.13, she burned her mouth, having been fooled by the cool cream, and started to untangle herself from the wife of lovely – *so lovely* – Oliver.

At 17.25, a group of friends, who would have heaved equal and separate sighs of relief as her text message lit up their phones, and who were already populating her inbox with exclamation marks, had – without realizing – sent their last messages to their precious Judy.

The 17.37, crammed with damp commuters, glued its doors shut to queuers and flaggers until Harbour Bridge.

She generously overtipped the waitress as a karmic thank-you, jumped into a cab home, dropped her bag in the hall, discarded on the bedroom floor every stitch of clothing she was wearing, and crawled into bed, where she slept soundly until Oliver creaked into the room an hour later.

'Sweetheart? Are you OK?'

He looked at the woman he hoped had been spared. He remained completely silent but his smile and stroking hand said: *I'm going to whisk you away to a place where we'll make a Sophie or Jack. You'll call me at work about a blue line and I'll take the rest of the day off. I'll announce it at a party fuelled with all the good reds I bought as investments. I know, now. I know.*

He didn't know, though.

'Hi. Sorry. I was knackered. I just wanted to sleep. What time is it?'

'Are you OK, Jude?'

'Yes. Just … a bit … What time is it?'

'Seven. I've said we'll go down to the pub for eightish. Celebrate. Is that OK?'

'God, Oli. Do we have to?'

'Come on! We've all been on tenterhooks. We could do with a drink and a laugh. Yes?'

She rolled out of bed, and pulled on the first dress she saw. By eight, they'd washed down an unremarkable dinner with something chilled and white. Oliver had talked animatedly between and during mouthfuls. Judy had nodded, smiled, released only the most carefully chosen words, and even conceded two or three little laughs. Sipping didn't seem to quell her overwhelming panic, so she had allowed herself the odd gulp while her husband focused on spearing the last few slippery leaves on his plate.

Oliver put his hand on the small of Judy's back as they stepped over the threshold. The pub wasn't as busy as she'd feared, and she immediately spotted her friends' grins lighting up the far corner. Even from a distance she could see Gina had been crying. Oliver made straight for the bar as Judy walked over to them, trying to smile. Min launched at her, all skinny arms and smacking kisses, while the others waited their turn. Paul had been trying to stop himself looking at women's breasts all evening, but allowed himself a moment on Judy's and Min's squashed up together.

Once Min released her grip, she cupped her hands around Judy's face. 'Hey, despite occasional evidence to the contrary, our Judy's "completely normal". Who knew?' The egg whites were now history, long forgotten.

More hugging. Cheers. Shuffling of bottoms to make room for their normal friend. She edged in next to Gina and squeezed her hand. Gina wiped a fast tear away. 'No crying, OK? I'm OK, OK?' A nod, another tear.

Judy looked around the table at their friends. 'OK, here's the deal. I don't want to talk about my right breast all night. Or the left one, to be honest. I just want to say I never want to go through that again, and I'm on large G-and-Ts all night, thank you!'

On cue, Oliver placed a large Tanqueray and tonic on the table. 'Yes, we're under strict orders, people. No talking about my wife's breasts tonight!'

'Anyway,' said Judy, changing the subject before anyone could alight on it, 'I want to hear all about the big weekend.' She looked at Rob. 'How did it go? Have you been welcomed into the bosom of the Chows?' Min's grandparents were on one of their rare visits to the UK, and had insisted on meeting Rob properly this time.

Rob stretched his arms out into a big open shrug. 'No. Can you believe it?'

Min laughed. 'Well, not exactly welcomed, but it went OK.'

'Min's grandparents are convinced I'll never be able to support us and our many, many future children.'

'Well, Mum and Dad tried to defend you. You shouldn't have said I earned twice as much as you!'

'I'm thrilled that you earn twice as much as me. I thought they'd be impressed that your business was going so well. Anyway, how was I supposed to respond to subtle enquiries about how much a gallery marketing officer earns "these days"?'

'Well, at least you turned up, Rob. I haven't seen George all weekend,' said Gina. All eyes were now on their friend with the pillar-box-red hair that clashed beautifully with her purple and green dress. Despite a series of disastrous relationships, Gina had retained a sense of optimism and enthusiasm for men, particularly medics and other clever buggers.

'Oh, very poor form from the new boyfriend,' said Oliver. 'I didn't like him, anyway.'

'He's joining us later,' said Gina.

'Oh, George, you say? Oh, yes, George, I like him!' Oliver laughed and winced behind a strategically placed beer mat.

Min grimaced. 'Oh, no! I thought you were supposed to be spending the weekend together. Weren't you cooking your aubergine thing for him?'

Gina smoothed down her dress, almost pretending to be distracted. 'I did. Then I froze it. *I'll* eat it.'

'You froze it? I'd have posted it through his letterbox!' Min continued, 'We all know junior doctors are overworked, Gina, but he almost never comes out, and when he does, he leaves early. He didn't even show up for Paul's birthday party. What's the betting we'll not see him tonight, either?'

Oliver stepped in to defuse the situation. 'Well, maybe he thinks we're a tedious lot who bug him about our minor ailments all evening rather than make a move for the bar. Now, more drinks? Same again, everyone?'

Min patted her barely rounding belly. 'Oh, yes, more orange juice – bring it on.'

Later, Gina would splosh a blot of red wine on that lovely cream coat of Min's; a regrettable accident, of course. The act would not be out of loyalty to George, or even the other men who'd not turned up, remembered they had a wife the morning after the night before, or tried it on with her sister or her friends, but in defence of her right to have faith in this one, the next one, and the one after.

Jen arrived, like a wasp at a picnic. She leaned across the table towards Paul, flashing the bar staff, and mouthed, quite unnecessarily, that she was going to the loo. He gave her the thumbs-up sign. She made her way across the pub, like a new kitten, skittering on perfectly solid ground. She tugged at her skirt hem and scratched at her thigh. She was a wreck. Paul was grateful he didn't have to be embarrassed in the company of his friends, and tried not to think about what anyone else thought.

By nine, Judy's friends had purged themselves of platitudes. She drank in their benign smiles and secretly stored them.

They all left the pub together and peeled off down their various sodium-lit streets and cul-de-sacs. Most houses were dark by closing time, curtains drawn, gates shut. The oldest residents could be identified by the empty milk bottles on their doorsteps. A man stood at his front door smoking his last cigarette of the day while his small excitable dog peed in the gutter, its back end temporarily obscured by its own steam. The standard greeting – 'Right' – was exchanged as the friends walked past him. Cats leaped and curled around in the dark, hiding under cars as the group approached, only the brave emerging for strokes and alcohol-fuelled petting. Tonight's rain wasn't worth commenting upon, and certainly prompted no hoods or umbrellas. Constellations of raindrops sat on people's heads and coats like hundreds of tiny transparent berries, too small even to roll.

When they arrived home, Oliver was in ebullient form. He tried to speak while brushing his teeth, splashing syllables and gesticulating while Judy hid behind cleanser-smeared palms. He spat out the last of his plaque and continued as if she had heard every word so far: 'And, if we go in two weeks, it'll tie in with my birthday. I've always fancied Prague.'

'Prague?'

'It doesn't have to be Prague. Paris. Madrid. Mi-lan-o! Or New York if you want to stretch it out a bit – say, go for a week. Come on! Noo Yawk for a week? Jump up and down a bit!'

She remained seated on the edge of the bed, hugging her knees. 'Do you remember Hannah Fisher?'

Oliver wasn't thrown by the non sequitur. 'No. Do I get three guesses?'

'What's above our mantelpiece, Oliver?'

'Damp?'

There wasn't a house in the street without a damp patch.

'Covering the damp patch.'

27

'Oh, yes. Hannah Fisher. Terrible signature, good use of colour.'

Judy straightened up and put her feet flat on the floor. 'She always said she wanted to be an artist. Even at school, when the teachers used to go on at her to concentrate on getting her maths and English, she'd be a right determined little sod.' She undid and rewound a covered elastic band around a doubled-over ponytail at the nape of her neck. 'I used to look at her and wonder where she got that strength from. You know, just to sit there and look the teachers in the eye and say, "Actually …"' She picked cotton balls from a plastic bag and started to run them over her face, revealing flushed trails of skin. '"Actually, I know exactly where I'm going, thanks. And I won't *need* to know about quadratic equations or split infinitives to get there." She'd sit up straight and just do this little thing with her jaw – just set it in position – and she was immovable. I'd be in awe of her. I didn't have a *clue* what I wanted to do, except pass maths and English at all costs. And now she's got a great big four-thousand-pound painting covering our damp patch, and God knows how many other damp patches all over the world, and spends half her time in Ibiza being "inspired by the light".'

There followed the longest silence of the evening. It took Oliver a full eight seconds to respond, during which time he tried to judge the mood. Once he realized he couldn't gauge it, he stuck with what he hoped was light and engaging.

28

'What *is* a split infinitive, anyway? I've never understood that. And what …' he knelt at her feet and kissed her knees '… does this have to do with New York?'

'Well, it's just … I don't know what we're celebrating, really,' she said.

He stopped kissing. 'Are you kidding me? We're celebrating the fact that your *terrifying* little lump turns out to be an inconvenience, not a life-threatening illness that could have cut you down in the prime of your life. That you're alive, Jude. That the diagnosis, in case you forgot, was normal.'

She closed her eyes. 'That doctor was spot on. I'm normal. It's not what I set out to be, but it's what I am. A hundred per cent normal.'

'That's what we're celebrating!'

'*I* want to be inspired by the light, Oli.'

OK, he could solve that one. Buying plane tickets, booking a hotel. That was right up his street. 'Right! Right. We'll go to Ibiza, then. Anywhere you want. Yes? Yes?'

She wondered where to start. He wanted to please her, to make things right, but he didn't have a clue. This time last night he had stroked and spooned her to sleep, and she had been grateful for every second until sleep had taken her. 'Yes, fine. I'm sorry. I'm really sorry. It's just been a bit of a day.'

Midnight. Air whistled almost imperceptibly over Oliver's flaccid tongue as Judy gazed into the shadowy middle distance, her bottom nestled into the small of his back. The golden light from a street lamp leaked through the curtains shyly gilding the room's jutting corners and sharp edges. A fleeting urge to store every shape she could make out was replaced by the thought that she'd never again tread the neural pathways that led to them. She had disengaged and all she had to do now was disentangle.

CHAPTER 6

Oliver was the kind of man women fell in love with, rather than fancied, at first sight. He had the frame of a rugby player, but not the temperament or the muscle. He looked like a man who *could* change a spare tyre but preferred not to. He had the creamy, middle-class skin of a (mostly organic) five-a-day man, and if you looked into his eyes long enough, you could see his Amazon password, his weakness for the white four inches above a stocking top, and where all the Christmas presents were hidden. His nose pointed to a mouth that grinned more than it kissed, but did both with irresistible ease. He was the kind of man parents hope their daughters will marry.

Judy got up for work the next morning because she didn't yet have the words not to. Occasionally, sentences that seemed as though they might do the job would form, but they took her breath away. Anyway, the routine of pulling on whites, greys and blacks and cogging through the day felt safer now she had decided to leave it all behind.

Some weeks passed.

'Don't worry too much about reading this right now. It's just to give you an idea of what we'll be doing this term. Can I just have a show of hands from those who already play an instrument?' Judy counted nine and realized that more than half of this cohort would need to endure bleeding fingertips or sore tendons before progressing to the next level.

She smiled at a teenaged girl whose woollen scarf obscured most of her face. 'What's your name?'

'Anna.'

'Anna, what do you play?'

The girl silently held up a violin case.

'Violin, good. To what grade?'

'Oh, I'm pretty much self-taught. My sister got me started. I don't read music at all.'

'OK, thank you, Anna.'

Next, Judy turned her attention to the only person sitting on a desk. His right arm was resting on an upright guitar case, and he looked like this term's hard work. 'Please – take a seat. I guess you play guitar. What's your name?'

'Chris MacLeod. Acoustic and electric. I'm sort of semi-pro. I earn most of my living from gigs but don't actually read music, so that's why I'm here.'

He looked like he hadn't seen the inside of a classroom for at least twenty years.

'Great, thank you, Chris. And those of you who have portable instruments, please do bring them in if you can.'

Judy raised her eyebrows and tilted her face upwards to invite the last of the nine to speak. No response.

'You play?'

'Yes,' he said.

'What's your name? What do you play?'

'Jon. Guitar.'

'Great. Do you have one?'

'Yep.'

'Good. Well, maybe you could bring it in next week, yes?'

'Well, it's more my brother's than mine. Well, his wife's.'

'Oh, OK,' said Judy. 'Can you borrow it?'

'I don't think she'd like me to bring it in here, but I can use it if I go round to their place.'

'OK, well, you have access to one, at least. Great.'

'Well, they live back up north now.'

OK, I've lost interest. I'm leaving soon anyway. You'll end up with Higgins, who'll recommend surgical spirit for your fingertips and Nurofen for your precious little tendons but wouldn't know a beautifully played passage if it hit him right in the rostromedial prefrontal cortex.

'Inverness ...'

She looked around for the projector she'd ordered. Facilities Management had decided she couldn't have one because it was about time these so-called academics understood that

33

multimedia presentations delivered via a Smartboard were the minimum expected standard, these days. She improvised for an hour drawing quavers, crotchets and clefs on the whiteboard, rubbing out too-long stems with the pad of her thumb. She realized, as she drew another stave, that she had just enough music tutor left in her to last for the rest of the day. Having given her students a fifteen-minute break, she gathered up her notes and headed for the photocopier.

Judy had forgotten what it felt like to lock a classroom door feeling elated rather than jaded. She had forgotten what it was like to see a class full of promise rather than problems.

Enough.

'A bit disorganized for you, Judith. Last-minute photocopying.'

'Sod off, Paul.'

'Now, now, no need for profanities in the first week of term. What's up?'

'Oh, you know. Our shiny brochure is attracting the usual rabble of lost souls looking for whatever insight we can give them in the space of the next ten weeks.'

'Oh, that.'

'And why aren't you in class?'

Paul pointed to a red-paint stain on his sweater. 'Bullet wound to the chest. Just been cleaning myself up. Left them doodling quick and dirty sketches of that fetid old cheese plant. Reckon I have another four minutes, tops, before they start going a bit Edvard Munch ...'

He mimed Munch's scream, mainly for his own amusement. Judy gathered up twenty-two copies of notes and nudged him out of the door. They fell into stride along the empty corridor.

'How you feeling, hon?' Paul's love for her was like a blanket.

'Awful. Lost. A complete fuck-up.'

'Doesn't anyone say "fine" any more?'

'I'm sick of all this … this …' She ran out of words so they started walking again.

'Is this your life guru talking?'

'He's a life *coach*. And, no, actually, it's my biopsy. They drew off litres and litres of normal. Imagine that.'

Judy considered letting her last class go early. In the end it ran over time, as she tried to imbue the students with stuff that Higgins didn't know was important. She abandoned her session plan and improvised for the rest of the lesson, encouraging her open-mouthed novices to delve between and beneath the notes on the stave, to play with them, shove them around a bit, dump them, then take up with them again in another bar. 'If you take only one thing away from this class,' she said, 'remember that Miles Davis said there are no mistakes. There are NO mistakes.'

Across town, Oliver had just discovered that a colleague's mistake was about to cost his law firm a lucrative contract. His assistant paused as she heard the unfamiliar sound of his raised voice behind the closed door.

At 28 Banks Road, a flame burst into life, and twelve radiators began the evening shift, warming high-ceilinged Victorian rooms. An hour later, Judy arrived home.

'I'm leaving. I need a break. I'm sorry, but …' She looked in the hall mirror as she tested the words. It would be at least an hour before Oliver arrived home, and at least a month before she'd be able to utter a single phrase to him that approximated the sense of what she wanted to say. A few weeks ago, she had bargained with the gods for her life, so it struck her as odd that it wasn't what she wanted at all. What she really wanted was to be alive. And she didn't know how or why that excluded Oliver, just that it did.

It wasn't his terrible ties or ghastly taste in films or the way he seemed unable to set down a hot cup without making a coaster out of an envelope or a supermarket leaflet. She accessed an image of him straight after sex, sweaty and tousled, moments before he smoothed down his hair and rearranged his features into a smile. She didn't know if that glimmer of blissed-out ease was the real Oliver or the secret Oliver. Whatever it was, a glimmer wasn't enough.

It seemed callous to stand barefoot and scrape away at carrot skin as she planned the breaking of her husband's heart. She despatched a slew of sliced carrots into a saucepan and made a start on blunting a handful of green beans. She held a bunch in both hands under the cold tap, rolling them between her palms past the point where her fingers grew painful from the increasingly icy water. Oliver's key turned in the lock and she picked up the knife.

'Jude?'

'In the kitchen.'

'Ooh, it's pouring down out there!' He shrugged off his raincoat, placing it on the worktop, and slowly unwound his scarf from his neck as he kissed the back of her head. 'How are you?'

'Fine.'

'Well, the big news of the day is that Simon has probably cost us the Regent account – minimum – and we'll be lucky if they don't sue us. I had him in my office today, and he couldn't even understand what the problem was. I said, "Simon, this is serious, we have given them misleading information that could cost them, not to mention us, a bloody fortune," but he didn't get it.'

He loosened his tie but didn't remove it.

'Tuna OK?'

'Yeah. Honestly, I've had it up to here with him. Anthony wanted me to go easy on him – I think he has a soft spot for him – but if we let this go, it's the thin end of the wedge.'

Judy put everything on to cook and levered herself up to sit on the worktop. Oliver hated it when she did that, as well she knew. She scrutinized him. For all this big talk, he wasn't a tough guy: Simon was safe.

'How long will the tuna be? Have I got time to change?'

No, Oliver, it's too late. 'Yes. Ten minutes.'

The phone rang. She hoped Oliver would pick it up, but after the fifth ring, she reached for it. It was Min. She sounded down. Judy flicked the tuna steaks over, poured a little salt into the carrot water, pulled two plates out of the cupboard and made sympathetic noises.

'What do you think really, Jude?' asked Min. 'Should I just say something?'

She'd lost track. 'I don't know.'

'Are you OK?'

'Fine.'

'Why don't you come over tonight?'

She thought about her options: a night in hearing more about Simon's shortcomings from Oliver, or a night out half listening to Min's perceived problems. 'Sure. I'll be over later. About eight-ish.'

The more she saw of other people, the more isolated she felt. She wondered if anyone had noticed that she really didn't care about stretch marks, incompetent colleagues, timetable mix-ups, the weather or the credit crunch. Some people didn't look for a response to their blathering. They would orate as though they were the subject of an in-depth interview, expecting interest (fascination, even) and punctuating every few sentences with unsolicited revelations about what made them tick. 'I'm very territorial,' they would explain, completely excusing their breathtaking hostility towards a colleague who had dared to perch on their chair for a moment. 'I'm just a party person,' the lush whose photocopied arse graced the staffroom noticeboard, would trill shamelessly. And if you could get someone on to the subject of their irritable bowel or dairy allergy, it could go on for hours.

Judy was relieved to discover that, if one nodded and made certain sounds in roughly the right gaps, people generally carried on regardless. Even tears, she found, could be handled with the simple offer of a tissue and a gently stroked hand. She had almost stopped talking completely. Hardly anyone had noticed.

That night, Min talked about how she felt Rob had been a bit distant since they'd found out she was pregnant, unlike her parents, who had no intention of keeping any sort of distance now a grandchild was imminent. The conversation was one-sided and loaded, a fishing expedition in part, but Judy didn't mind. She cared enough to nod and make sounds but didn't have the strength to defend her brother. She tuned out several times, managing to stay alert for just long enough to get the gist of most of what Min was saying.

She didn't notice she was drifting off to sleep, and Min only noticed when one of her extended gripes was met with silence.

An hour or so later, Rob arrived home. He saw his sister snailed up on the sofa. Min was next to her, reading a magazine.

'What's going on?'

'She fell asleep,' said Min. 'We need to call Oliver.'

Minutes later, Oliver led his wife to the car as if she were a child. If she stayed, if she blocked her ears and eyes and heart, if she took the path of least resistance, these people would guide her around every bump in her path; they would be there at every step, north, south, east and west, of her life, guarding her from pain, soothing her to acquiescent quietude. She had never nursed as much as a scraped knee on her own. There had always been someone to reach for the real and metaphorical plasters.

Once home, Oliver removed Judy's coat and shoes and put her to bed, all the while assuring her that everything was going to be OK.

CHAPTER 7

'I THINK YOU'RE SUFFERING from anxiety, and I'm going to recommend you take a couple of weeks off, at the very least. You need to come back in a fortnight and we'll check how you're getting on.'

Dr Kahan had seen her through every scribbled jotting of her medical history, from chickenpox to the Pill. His starchy whites had long been replaced by pushed-up blue shirt sleeves and chinos, and she noticed his sinewy forearms. He was still a fine violinist in his spare time, mainly Klezmer music, and had once asked her advice about whether he should take up the accordion. She wondered whether he'd done so, but felt it wasn't the time to ask. That sort of chat seemed to sit better in the context of a sore shoulder or a sprained ankle.

'I can also prescribe something for the anxiety – something that will—'

'No, thanks. Really. I just need a couple of weeks off, I think.'

She stood up to leave, and stumbled against the chair, scraping it back until it hit the wall. He caught hold of her elbows and gently led her into a sitting position again. He slid his hands down her arms and cupped her hands. She had a vague idea that doctors weren't supposed to do such things any more, but his palms felt solid and sure against the back of her hands, and his thumbs in the centre of her palms pinioned her into making direct eye contact. She fantasized, for a moment, that he had the power to make everything all right.

'Judith ...'

She left the surgery with a prescription that she later shredded.

Doc gave me 2wk sick note and said to take hol. J.

She selected 'Oli' on her iPhone and hit send, then surfed for ideas, for something to jump out at her. She wanted space to think. She wanted to be around unfamiliar people or perhaps nobody. She panicked at the prospect of sitting behind the weekend papers hearing Oliver criticize someone's unconvincing song choices on *Desert Island Discs*, week in, week out, for years and years. By the time he arrived home that evening, she'd booked herself on a women's retreat. It was a few weeks away, but it was a start.

She didn't know how to arrange sick leave because she couldn't remember ever having done it before. She'd had the odd cold or migraine that had necessitated a day or two off, a couple of missed lessons here and there, but she'd never had to hand over a class completely. It was liberating and frightening. She rang Audrey, the faculty secretary, and tried to explain her situation.

'My GP says I should take at least a couple of weeks but he says it could be longer.'

Audrey mentally scanned the music staff, and stopped at Higgins. He was always up for extra work.

'I'm sorry, Audrey, I know this will mean extra work for you – finding someone to teach my classes ...'

'Oh, no, don't even think about it. Can you tell us what it is? Is it anything serious?'

'I'm not well,' was the only reply she could manage.

She was crying when she put the phone down. She'd hoped to have the feeling of release that one gets after ringing in sick, but instead she felt in limbo, as if she'd just stubbed her toe and was now waiting for the consequence to kick in.

'A retreat?' Oliver crinkled his face. In less than a decade he'd be considering Botox for the mess he was making of it.

'It's an all-women environment, where women ... come together ... and ... well ...' Judy had very little idea of what would happen; all she knew for sure was that she was going.

'Bloody hell, Jude! It'll be full of hairy-legged aromatherapists!'

'I just want some time to …' She wanted some time to think. She wanted to breathe different air. She wanted to be around people who didn't add 'and Oliver' when they talked about her, people who didn't know her parents' names, people who lived too far away to pop in for coffee because they were 'just passing'. She wanted to listen to women with unfamiliar accents talking about stuff she knew nothing about.

'They'll have you chanting and chucking out your eyeliner!'

No chance. The eyeliner wasn't going anywhere. 'I know what you mean, but I don't think—'

'Before you know it, you'll buying something fetching in tie-dye from the on-site shop!' He was on a roll.

'Oliver.' She found herself disconcertingly engaged with him now. 'Please.'

His grin tightened into a rueful smile. 'I'm sorry, babe. I just can't imagine you on a women's retreat, that's all. You don't really go in for that kind of stuff, normally.'

'No.'

'But I'm one hundred per cent behind you. Seriously, I am. When is it?'

'A few weeks' time.'

'Right. Good. Good. OK. Fancy a glass of wine?'

CHAPTER 8

JUDY'S PARENTS SMILED OUT from a collection of decades-spanning black-and-white photographs on the piano. Barbara and Ray looked like background extras from *Mad Men*, in that they were good-looking enough to be on set but not quite glamorous enough to be given lines. If you wanted to be picky, Barbara was a little heavy on the hips even for those hourglass times, and Ray's teeth were not exactly the stuff of Central Casting. Despite that, they were a fine-looking couple as long as Barbara wasn't giving Ray too much to smile about.

There was much jostling for space on the piano: Judy in her pram, in pigtails, in school uniform, head down in family shots during the teenage years, smiling a full Duchenne on her wedding day with Oliver; Rob at similar stages, minus the pigtails and wedding day. And there were others: grandparents, aunts and uncles, cousins. Each photograph had been inexpertly slotted into a frame, usually by Ray. Some were lucky enough to land straight first time. Others lived with their heads permanently cocked, as though questioning why the framer hadn't just given it one more try. Straight or otherwise, Barbara took off and polished each frame every Saturday morning.

Occasionally, an event would call for another photo to be framed, which necessitated some rearrangement, usually a shift backwards for someone. It had taken time but the seventies pictures had been heartened to see that the black-and-whites from the sixties had recently been moved forward to the front row. There were murmurings from the ranks that beige, brown and orange were set for a similar comeback any year now.

Judy had expected to find both her parents at home, but Rob had gone out with Dad to a local football match. Barbara had taken the opportunity to throw away a stack of newspapers that her husband had been building by the side of the bed for several weeks, and to vacuum the mattress. When she was home alone, her fault-finding radar bleeped with delight at potential clearouts and deep-cleaning jobs.

'I think you should go and see Dr Kahan and get him to prescribe a little something for you,' said Barbara, pouring a steaming gush of water into a waiting teapot.

'I've already been, Mum. And I don't want anything like that!' replied Judy.

'Like what? Listen – you're lucky to live in an age when they'll write you out a prescription, my girl. You know what happened to Auntie Elsie! She had no say. One minute, she was peeling potatoes and the next she was strapped into a long-sleever and carted off!'

'Mum, I am not about to be carted off.'

'That's what I'm saying, Judith! You won't be carted off because you have other options. Let me talk to Dr Kahan for you—'

'You're not speaking to anyone on my behalf, Mum. Leave it!'

Judy channelled her inner teacher. There was a brief silence.

'What are you cooking for Oliver tonight?'

'What?'

'I have some nice steak going off in the fridge. Your father says he can't face it. It has a best-before date of … Let me check …' Barbara walked towards the fridge.

'Don't check! I don't want the steak!'

'Well, have you a better idea? What man doesn't want a steak when he gets home?'

'I don't know, Mum. And I don't know what Oliver wants. Perhaps you could ask him. Would you like his office number and you could call him out of a meeting?'

'There's no need to speak to me like that,' said Barbara, sharply. ' I'm offering you best rump. If you don't want it, just say no.'

'No.'

'Well, it's your loss.'

Barbara poured the tea into two saucered cups. 'Will you have a biscuit, at least?' A peace offering.

'Yes, please. A biscuit would be lovely,' said Judy, softening.

'I have the Party Rings or the Rich Tea.' Her mother had been buying Party Rings since Judy's sixth birthday.

'A Party Ring.' Judy snapped the biscuit in two and placed one half iced side down on her tongue – only once the icing was dissolving did she bite. After several years of research, she had categorically ascertained that there was no better way to eat a Party Ring.

'Auntie Jo was asking after your ...' Barbara concentrated on the tricky dunk of a Rich Tea.

Judy swallowed the last of her biscuit. 'Breast?'

'I know what it is, Judy. I have two of my own. She was asking after your health.'

'Physical or mental?'

'She just wanted to know if you were all right. We've all been very concerned, darling.'

'I know, Mum. I know you have.' She stroked Barbara's hand. 'So was I. I was concerned for *myself*. But it's just made me think ...'

'Well, try not to, darling.'

Later that evening, as Judy grilled best rump that was a day past its sell-by date, Rob called her. 'I need to speak to you about Dad.'

It was an ominous opening that continued in the same vein. 'I think he's getting worse at remembering stuff.'

Judy turned the heat down and started to make salad dressing, one-handed. 'How much worse? He's *never* remembered any birthdays if you're still sulking about that,' she replied, drizzling olive oil into a jug.

'Not birthdays and shit. People's names. Footballers' names. Important goal scorers.'

Judy laughed, mainly to keep the inevitable at bay. 'Well, if that's a sign of—'

'I'm serious, Jude. I think we should tell Mum.'

'She knows! She's with him all the time, Rob. What's there to say?'

'That he's getting worse. That he's acting a bit funny as well. Singing over the news and stuff.'

'Singing?'

'Not just that. You need to have a word. She'll listen to you.'

'She already thinks I'm about to be carted off in a white van, and now you want me to tell her that I think something's wrong with Dad because he's singing over the headlines? She doesn't listen to me any more than she listens to you or Dad.'

There was a moment's silence.

'Well, let's tell her together,' he said. 'It's not just the singing, Jude …'

'Oh, Christ! OK, tell me exactly what he's having trouble with.'

So Rob explained. He told her how, on the car journey to the football match, Dad had burst into song – remembering every word of a Frank Sinatra tune that he reprised over and over, in the car, across the car park, through the turnstile and on to the terraces, until the players came on to the pitch. How he could remember all the details of the 1966 World Cup but had forgotten that Min was pregnant. How he thought David Cameron was some bloke who ran a café and record shop in Deansgate. Serious, unmistakable stuff.

The next day, Judy and Rob arrived at their parents' house together and asked Barbara to take a seat because they wanted to talk to her. Barbara had never liked it when people asked her to take a seat. She leaned against the kitchen cupboards instead, and listened to her children tell her what she already knew.

'Oh, for goodness' sake, you two! I thought it was something serious! I thought he'd flashed someone or something!'

'Flashed someone? Mum, what are you talking about?' asked Judy.

'Well, Uncle Alex started flashing. People were very understanding, though. Poor Auntie Maud was mortified but even the local bobbies took it in their stride. I think your cousin Geoffrey used to goad him into it sometimes.'

Judy tried not to think about genetics.

'You think Dad's got what Uncle Alex had?' asked Rob, trying not to think about genetics.

'I don't know, love. We all get muddled. I left my hairspray in the fridge last week.'

'Oh, God,' groaned Rob. 'I can see how this is going to end. Dad getting put on some list for dropping his kecks in the Trafford Centre. It'll be all over the papers, I can see it now.'

'All right, Nostradamus, don't get carried away,' said Judy. 'Mum, I think we should take him to the doctor. Just for a check-up.'

'And what good would that do, hey? They'd just tell him he was getting older and that this is to be expected and—'

'No!' said Judy. 'No, they wouldn't, Mum! They'd do tests. He's been struggling for ages. We should get tests done now.'

Barbara made one last valiant attempt to preserve the status quo. 'Tests? What for? I hardly know what David Cameron's doing myself. Do you? Maybe he *should* be running a café on Deansgate. You two should be trying to sort your own lives out instead of—'

Ray appeared in the doorway. 'I've been asleep again. What's everyone doing in here? Is someone going to make me a cup of tea?'

Barbara ushered him to her vacated seat and made more tea for everyone. Judy and Rob offered him the plate of biscuits and asked how he'd slept.

'Lying down,' he replied, stuffing custard creams into his pockets.

Dr Kahan opted for a new type of screening process to assess Ray for the possibility of Alzheimer's. He took plenty of time beforehand to explain how this new test could throw up false positives but that it was still better at identifying the disease than the older test.

Barbara leaned forward as the doctor spoke, as though her proximity to him might somehow save them from what was about to unfold. She scanned his kind face for traces of a reassuring smile, but no.

Ray nodded, eyebrows raised, but he was actually trying to read what the certificates on the wall said. They made him think of Judy's graduation. He remembered it so clearly. They had been running late – Judy had taken a long time getting ready. He had joked that she would be shrouded in a gown anyway. There had been a near miss on the motorway, a blowout. He'd handled the car like a professional, steering steadily towards the hard shoulder. He'd herded his family up a grass verge and had walked confidently to the roadside phone, cars whizzing past his ears making his jacket flap open. The memory of the sounds of car engines and tyres on tarmac drowned Dr Kahan's voice.

CHAPTER 9

THE MOMENT FOR A serious conversation with her family had passed. Mum and Dad clearly didn't need more upset and Rob would probably blow his top, then climb up on to the high horse he kept tethered on standby. Her friends were unlikely to understand. What was she going to say? *The biopsy turned out OK so I'm leaving while I have the chance?* Or: *I know we all love Oliver, but I'm going to break his heart – so would you mind looking after him while I swan off to get my kicks elsewhere?* It seemed easier to … well, actually, none of it seemed easy. She texted Gina.

Hi. Fancy meeting up? A quick chat?

They arranged to meet at the Tudor, a brasserie that had once been a thriving pub and music venue before the smoking ban. The new owners had tried to give a nod to the building's musical roots by framing whimsical hand-made posters of long-gone local bands like Eskimo Folk Tales and Easter. If you looked closely enough, you could see the drawing-pin holes in the corners of each poster. And the cleaners swore they sometimes heard the faint jangle of guitars as they locked up for the night.

Gina was tiny – the complete opposite of how people perceived and remembered her. An enormous presence emanated from her ballerina-like physique because almost everything about her seemed to be glued at maximum volume. The first thing that struck most people about her was her ever-changing hair, always dyed in colours one wouldn't normally associate with actual hair: blue, purple, green, pink. She kept it short so that she could shave it all off at whim and start again the next week. Her face was a work of art, in which the only constant was her immovable (first coat, blot, powder, second coat, blot) Russian Red lipstick, which often compelled people to watch as well as listen to what she had to say, doubling the impact of any articulated thought or idea, however fleeting. Waiting staff would seat her in restaurant corners because she might just rowdy up, or at least disturb, the room if positioned among other diners. Bank managers would take one look at her and assign their underlings to deal with her pleas for a bigger overdraft. Shop assistants fell silent while they served her, barely able to ask her to punch in her PIN. Yet, inside … Inside Gina beat a heart of such sensitivity that she was almost moved to tears every time she bought a *Big Issue*. She would get on her hands and knees and *blow* ants away from her doorstep until she had to reach for her inhaler. When she bleached her sink, she would send a trickling stream of lukewarm water down the plughole first, to warn anything bigger than bacteria to get out of the way. She had been Judy's best friend since they had met on the first day of primary school.

One of Judy's most vivid memories was from a morning almost thirty years ago. She had been running around the playground with a group of girls when Gina suddenly fell down and started to gasp desperately for air. The other girls started to cry and scream, but Judy had been unable to move, and stood transfixed as each second dragged another bit of life from the focus of the ghoulish scene. Eventually, Mr Douglas emerged from the school and ran across to them, trailing the smell of pipe smoke from the staffroom along two corridors and out into the playground. Mrs Fish followed, clip-clopping across the tarmac and flagstones, shedding crumbs from her bosom for a watchful crow, and made it her duty to shoo away the gawpers and yowlers.

The ambulance raced through the town, its siren alerting polishing mums whose trains of thought switched to sickly relatives and neighbours. Men in factories, who were afforded the tiniest sound bite, wondered about bottles of Valium in bathroom cabinets and their sons' motorbike brakes. Children touched their collars, reciting the rhyme that would surely protect them from a death surrounded by experts.

Gina breathed deeply from the mask that was immediately placed over her face, and her airways opened and relaxed. A flush of colour returned as she smiled at Judy. Everything was going to be all right.

Some years passed.

'Hello, darling! Ugh, I've got too many layers on!' As she hugged Judy, Gina eyed the display of cakes and pastries over her shoulder. 'Ooh, I'm in desperate need of a big wodge of carrot cake. Will they serve just cake, do you think? On its own?' She shrugged off her coat and waved to a nearby waiter as though she was drowning. 'Excuse me! Can I get just cake? I only want cake.'

The waiter tried to persuade his colleague to attend to her – it wasn't his table and he was busy trying to remember the details of the order he'd just taken. He'd seen other waiting staff do this – take orders without writing them down. He was so impressed that every time he took an order from a table of fewer than four people, he would keep his pencil in his pocket. His hesitance resulted in the waving woman striding towards him.

'Hi! Can I get just cake?'

The waiter willed two soups of the day, a large green salad, no onions, the sea bass and the aubergine bake to stay in his head. 'Yes, of course. Someone will come and take your order.'

Not the answer she was looking for. She persisted: 'Oh, I know that, but I was wondering if you would serve *just* cake. On its own. Yes?'

Two soups of the day, a large green salad, no onions, the sea bass and the aubergine bake, two soups of the day, a large green salad, no onions, the sea bass and the aubergine bake. 'Yes, we will. If that's all you want. Someone will come and take your order soon.' *Two soups of the day, a large green salad, no onions, the sea bass … Shit.*

Gina managed to knock four chairs as she wove back to the table. 'I'm having the cake.' She grinned, and did a thumbs-up as though she'd just bribed the chef to make her a small batch of rose-petal *macarons*.

'I'm having a nightmare. Sit down!' said Judy.

They sat side by side, leaning into each other like sisters, looking out of the window, at each other and out of the window again. Even when they were watching strangers pass by, they knew what each other's face looked like. They didn't need the clues that come with scrutinizing the twitch of a lip or the squint of an eye to know what the other was thinking. Over tea and barely shared carrot cake, Judy circled around the real issue for a while, remaining vague until it looked like Gina might start harping on about George.

'Have you ever felt like you want to do something really bad and you can't explain why?'

Asking Gina that was like asking a child what they liked best about sweet shops.

'Absolutely. Do you remember that guy I met on holiday that time? That Richard guy? You remember, the one with the …' Gina was off. She recounted how Richard had semicircled around a bonfire on a perfect Mediterranean night to tell her how beautiful she looked in the light of the fire. She remembered how, as he'd nuzzled into her neck, he described how 'very attached' he was to his girlfriend back home yet 'There he was, snogging me like it was an Olympic sport. And when I found him on Facebook and saw his girlfriend's page ...' She stopped. Judy was staring into her coffee.

'I'm thinking of leaving Oliver. Leaving here. *Leaving* leaving.' She had somehow managed to time this grim announcement between the café's music tracks, like some acutely depressed wedding DJ. If anyone was still talking in the café, they were doing it bloody quietly. Judy felt they had not only heard what she'd said but that they were now listening for her to carry on. She waited for the next track to start before continuing. 'I can't carry on with things the way they are.'

'What things? Have you met someone else?'

'No. God, no. I'd have told you if I had. Jesus, Gina. No, it's not that. I don't know what things exactly. I just want to leave.'

'Have you told Ol?'

'No.'

Gina sat with her hand across her mouth, as though she was stopping the wrong words tumbling out. It was as close to saying the right thing as she could get.

'I just need to talk to somebody about it because I'm going out of my mind.' Her voice started to falter. She swallowed the tears and grabbed Gina's hands. 'And I need you to promise me, Gina, that you won't say a word to anyone. Not even George. Not a word. OK?'

Gina nodded, wide-eyed.

Judy rewound to the night before the biopsy. She explained how she'd listened to Oliver snoring over her charcoal thoughts. How she'd been so still and quiet that she'd been almost dead anyway. How she loved babies but didn't want one of her own, let alone three. How there absolutely and definitely wasn't anyone else. No. How she knew that Oliver was lovely. Yes. How she knew he would be devastated. And how she was absolutely serious about leaving. Yes. For good.

'I just feel I'm wasting my life a bit, really. I feel like I'm stuck on some treadmill – I know that's a cliché but it's true, I do.'

'We all feel like that sometimes, though, Jude. Is it serious enough to want to leave everything behind? Not just Oliver, but everything.'

'What everything?'

'Well, your friends, for a start.'

'I don't mean ... I know I have friends here, but it's not like I'm moving to another planet. I'm just moving away from here. We'll still see each other.'

'Jude, I don't know where this has come from but can you not just ride it out for a bit? Most people feel like this at some point, but then they knuckle down again. It's not unusual. It passes. And people are not unhappy, generally, or they'd leave. You've never said to me that you're unhappy. This is all from out of the blue, as far as I can see. I think it will pass. Honestly, I do.'

'It's not wind, Gina. It won't just pass.'

'You don't even have to work, Jude! I mean, that's huge. I wish I didn't have to work. I have loads of stuff I'd rather be doing. You could just make music or do your art or ...'

Judy felt like she might snap, so she let Gina continue while she focused on the couple sitting at the next table, not talking, barely engaged with each other. If she had been there with Oliver, they would have at least been speaking.

'Gina, stop. Please. Be my friend. Let me talk to you about it, but don't try to keep me here.'

Gina started to cry a bit but not enough to draw more attention to herself. She would cry more later, once she was home and it had all started to sink in. Judy hugged her and told her everything would be all right, which was an absolute whopping great lie.

CHAPTER 10

O N SATURDAY MORNING JUDY took the tram into Manchester city centre. She had inched slowly from bed, silently concertinaing the duvet towards Oliver, barely breathing so that he would stay in his dreams. She landed in town early – any later and she would have had to snake along Deansgate, darting between slow-moving families and strolling lovers. As she walked up the stairs of the Cornerhouse for breakfast, she reminisced about the early days of her relationship with Oliver, before they were married. She smiled into her coffee as she remembered the night they'd seen Kieslowski's *Three Colours* trilogy downstairs from where she now sat. Reclining with their faces tipped up to the screen, they'd luxuriated in the beauty of Juliette Binoche, Julie Delpy and Irène Jacob. It had gone midnight when the final credits rolled and the ushers opened the side exits. There had been an almost palpable wave of excitement as the audience gradually spilled out into unexpected snowfall, with flakes the size of marshmallows.

Have a gd wknd! I'll take care of Ol and u take care of u. Paul x

Deal. How u? Jx

Paul didn't respond right away. Text wasn't a suitable medium for telling anyone that Jen was pregnant – and that, no, it wasn't his. Or for telling his friend in need that he'd been accepted to coach at a summer soccer camp in Brazil, and couldn't wait to leave.

The Manchester to Liverpool train was busy. As soon as the doors opened, families rushed on to secure table seats while teenagers lurked in doorways, blocking everyone's path. Judy tucked herself at the quietest end of a carriage.

What am I doing on a train going to a workshop where I won't fit in? Am I going to end up like one of those women who chucks her life up in the air and is still sitting surrounded by the rubble, babbling baby talk to a kitchen table full of cats years later? I could just get off the train and go shopping. There are everyone's Christmas presents to be bought and . . . Jesus, Christmas!

She thought about the huge bundle of mistletoe that everyone had kissed under last year. She'd carried it back from town on the bus, enjoying the smiles and cheeky comments from other passengers squiffy on their office-party drinks. It had dangled for a month or so from the ceiling light in the porch. Over the first couple of days, she had picked up the precarious pearly berries that had been shooshed from their branch by the top of the front door or poked off by closing umbrellas. She'd kissed a lot under that mistletoe. Her mind wandered back to the last time she had really kissed Oliver. He had been so fed up at having to hang the buggering thing after a fucking long day that the last thing he'd wanted to do was kiss under it, thanks very much. Surely she'd kissed him – really kissed him – since then? It would have been New Year's Eve. That was nearly a year ago.

By the time Paul texted back, Judy was off the train and in a cab en route to a converted church in the heart of Liverpool.

More Jen shit. On way to footy. Am staying ur place 2nite. Ol bringing something vintage up from cellar! P xxx

Judy envied him the physical vigour of kicking a ball about for ninety minutes. Perhaps that was what she needed. Perhaps that was why Paul did it. God knows, he needed a physical outlet with all that pent-up anger and frustration. She hoped there would be boxing gloves and pads at the retreat. Or at least a ball.

There *were* balls, but they were enormous and one was expected to sit on them. Barefoot, she negotiated her way through the rubbery silver orbs to the friendliest-looking corner of the room. There, she sipped a cup of what had definitely been described to her as 'tea' and looked around her. There were no hairy legs to be seen, but there was a reassuring range of coloured toenails from coral to midnight blue. One woman did wear tie-dye, but it was a T-shirt, not a dress, with a fabulously Hirstesque diamanté relief skull grinning from it, like a third breast. Judy realized she would be happy to spend the weekend with any of the women she could see, including the one on tea-making duty whose talents obviously lay in other areas. Despite the ball-balancing, there was an ease in the room, as though they already knew that simply absenting themselves from daily life would restore them.

Olivia Thomas entered the room with the presence and glamour of a fifties starlet, minus the jewels. Judy had expected more of an earth-mother type, perhaps wearing a turban or a kaftan, but 'Liv' looked like she'd just hopped off the back of a Vespa and skipped in. She was a vision in black pedal pushers and a boat-necked black-and-white striped top; a ginger-haired Leslie Caron for the twenty-first century. Judy almost peeped to see if Gene Kelly was about to dance in behind her.

Liv launched into a sparky opening speech, which ended: 'This weekend is your adventure. Some of you will be feeling excited or nervous, some of you will have arrived here sad or wanting to make a change in your lives. It doesn't matter why you're here, I know that you'll all leave feeling better than you did when you arrived.' She laughed and actually did a little jump as she finished speaking, engendering a ripple of unexpected mini crushes throughout the room. By Sunday afternoon most of the women would be quite smitten with her.

In order to get the most out of the weekend, Judy had written a list:

1. Join in with everything except singing
2. Tell the truth
3. Don't make smartarse remarks about the activities to anyone else on the retreat
4. Try and get some quiet time alone
5. Turn mobile off until retreat ends – NO CHECKING AT LUNCHTIME!
6. Drink more water
7. Don't fall apart!

'OK, if you can bring your balance balls into a circle, we'll take a few minutes to introduce ourselves to each other.' Liv clearly expected the women to balance on the balls all weekend. Judy looked around the large hall for stacks of chairs and tables, but there were none.

A heavily pregnant woman started the circular process. 'I'm Abby, and I'm from North Wales, and I'm just hoping I don't burst this ball!' She let out a rolling gurgle of a laugh that invited anyone to join in. There was something alarmingly imminent about the sight of her laughing and squatting on the opaquing ball. 'I started maternity leave a week ago. I'm here because this will be my third child and I need some time to myself before I finally become a full-time mother and housewife for the next few months. My in-laws are looking after the kids and my husband's away on a walking weekend, so we're both hoping we'll feel great next week!'

Judy scrutinized Abby's round, clear face for discomfort, doubt, a shadow of uncertainty, but all she could glean was a bit of tiredness around her eyes. She seemed like the kind of woman who would grunt rather than scream a baby out, then latch it straight on to the breast, blood and all. Solid.

'OK, I'm Marta. I'm from Minnesota. I'm on a gap year. I've been in the UK for three months and I'm spending two weeks here in Liverpool, then going to Norway and Sweden. I liked the idea of a women's retreat because I'm travelling with two guys from my university and they're, like, driving me crazy!'

Too young to be uncertain, Judy thought. We know everything at that age.

'Hello, I'm Judy. I'm a music tutor. I work part time at a college and also see private students. I'm here because I ...' *Because I don't know what the hell I'm going to do with my life except smash it up and break people's hearts.* 'Because I'm at a bit of a crossroads, to be honest.' The bridge of her nose was tingling, and she could feel tears forming. She gave Liv a huge fake grin that said, 'Rescue me! Move on to the next person!'

'Thanks, Judy.' Liv smiled expectantly at the woman balancing next to Judy.

'I'm Harriet Booth. Everyone calls me Harry. I do whatever I can get paid for in the daytime, within reason, mainly designing websites for small businesses, and I work in a bar a couple of nights a week. I sing there one or sometimes two nights a week, but wish I could do more of that and less of everything else. My boyfriend lives just around the corner, so I spend most weekends here – I actually live in Edinburgh – and I'm here today because I saw it advertised outside a few weeks ago. And, like Judy, I'm at a bit of a crossroads. I'm wondering if I should move down here to be with my boyfriend or even go to London to try and do the singing full time.'

Judy was so grateful that all eyes were on Harry now that the need to cry subsided. Once the introductions were over, the activities started with a group meditation and a bit of chanting before lunch.

She found it comforting to be able to speak with people who had no expectations of her and no shared history – people who wouldn't hate her in a few weeks' time. She kept the tears at bay by offering half-truths across the table and concentrating on mouthfuls of the most delicious stuffed vine leaves. She washed down moments of rising panic with silky gulps of Liverpool tap water. She remembered that someone had once told her that, in order to keep attention away from your nerves, you should ask lots of questions. She was doing a pretty good job until Harry collared her.

'So. Do you want to talk about this crossroads you're at,' asked Harry, 'or are you still feeling a bit delicate?'

'No, I'm not delicate. I'm …' There were no vine leaves left and she'd surely pee on the spot if she drank any more water.

'It's just that I've been to things like this before, and I know that if you don't grab the opportunity, it's all a bit pointless, really,' said Harry.

'I'm leaving my husband.' It felt like she was trying on a dress that she suspected wouldn't hang very well once on.

'Oh. Right. Sorry.'

'No, it's fine,' she said, metaphorically adjusting the sleeves and doing a bit of a twirl in the mirror. 'I just came here to try and get my head around what I really should do, but I know what I should do. I just don't know if I can.'

'Does he know?'

'I'm not sure.'

Harry left a little gap for Judy to think. Then she said, 'You don't have to talk about it, obviously.'

'I'm not going to be able to explain any of this to my family, to his family, to our friends. Well, I've talked to one of my friends about it. Nobody else will understand and, if you met him, I'm not sure you would, either. He's a great guy and I love him, I really do love him, but I don't want to spend the rest of my life with him because ...' she paused and rubbed her temples '... because I'm now that woman who buys her CDs and clothes as part of the weekly grocery shop. And every single pair of knickers I currently own came in a pack of three and can be washed at high temperatures.'

Harry laughed.

'My life is perimetered in a square mile. My year is all mapped out from September to June. I've found myself dancing to the rhythm of about sixty supermarket shops a year, thirty term-time Monday mornings, nearly the same amount of faked orgasms because I'm too fucking tired to go for the real thing, a handful of black-tie events I have to smile through as "wife of Oliver", even though the Spanx will be cutting lines into me that'll still be there in the morning, and a conveyor-belt of birthday cakes that is speeding up with each passing year.' She took a deep breath. Once the truth starts to make its way out, there's no stopping it.

'Can I ask that you all come back to the main room in about five minutes, please?' shouted Liv, over the buzz of intense conversation.

Oliver was making the most of Judy's absence. The kitchen table was covered with butterflied newspaper sections. Buttery toast crumbs and globs of jam were spattered over the worktops along with dark crescents of discarded pizza crust. A block of French salted butter sweated on the chopping board.

He glugged most of a bottle of 1994 Château Lacoste Borie-Pauillac into two generous glasses, as though it were weekday plonk, and handed one to Paul. 'Here, get some of this down you.'

Paul had just told him that Jen was pregnant and that, no, it wasn't his.

'So, what's going to happen? I mean, have you discussed …'

'She's seeing a doctor in town on Monday. A private one. And she's going to find out how far gone she is and stuff – and then …' Paul shrugged matter-of-factly and swilled the wine around in his glass.

'An abortion?'

'I don't know.'

They both swigged the wine as they leaned against the table, side by side, and looked out of the kitchen window. It was raining hard now.

'She was stoned when I got in last night. Completely off her head. God knows what she'd been taking. No baby would stand a chance against all that.'

Oliver winced. 'What did she say?'

'She just … she just said she …' Paul shook his head and gnawed at a piece of hard skin on his thumb.

Oliver was out of questions so he tried to think of something comforting to say but ended up making murmuring sounds.

'And I could see, you know, when she walked from the bathroom to the bed, a … bump. She's all skin and bone, but there's this bump.' Paul spanned his hand across his belly. His nails were outlined with red paint.

'Shit.'

'Yeah.'

CHAPTER 11

MIN HAD HOPED THAT her relationship with Rob might strengthen during the pregnancy, and that the late-night texts – to which he responded only once she was out of sight – might stop. She had no doubt that they were from Carly, who worked as box-office manager at the same gallery as he did. Barely out of her teens, Carly was all gleaming teeth and gangly legs. She had a penchant for hot-pants worn with brightly coloured opaque tights in winter and bare, tanned legs in summer, and she had recently been dumped by her rugby-playing boyfriend. Rob had been adamant that he was merely a shoulder to cry on, and Min had believed him because that was the kind of guy he was.

She had tried to reassure herself that the source of her unease was raging pregnancy hormones and her long-standing insecurities. But when he touched her expanding belly, it felt like a hollow Hallmark gesture – not that she dared share her thoughts with anyone. She could figure out why he'd gone off sex but she wasn't sure if he was finding it as much of a struggle as she was.

The baby clothes, cot blankets, the furry rabbits that couldn't be picked up without being stroked against one's cheek piled up in a corner undisturbed by an inquisitive father-to-be. It wasn't that he had no interest in the baby – on the contrary – but it seemed that he was starting to think of Min not so much as his 'sex kitten' (he hadn't called her that – his secret nickname for her – in months) but more as a vessel in which to grow the new arrival. While she was flush with love and nesting instincts, he was frowning over school league tables, measuring the garden for a sandpit and trying to reconnect with his own dad. She wanted to believe it was his way of being excited about their new family unit, but all evidence suggested that, to Rob, it was just another project to be planned and milestoned.

He didn't seem unhappy, more disconnected. When he cooked – which was becoming more frequent – he presented the meal with a smile rather than a kiss, accompanied by banal physical flourishes and phrases like 'Bon appétit!' or 'Get it while it's hot!' Whenever she touched him, she found herself checking for signs that the old Rob was there, half expecting to find a hinged panel to reveal a Stepfordesque explanation of what was going on.

She didn't dare to wonder why he didn't leave his phone lying around any more – and she could hardly ask where it was. She tried to get around it one day by challenging him to a game of Scrabble – she had downloaded the app specifically to see his phone again – but he said he was too tired and was thinking of an early night. But not *that* kind of early night.

The idea that he'd been fiddling about in Carly's hot-pants exacerbated Min's already omnipresent nausea.

Rob tried his best to cope with Min's mood swings and general grumpiness, putting them down to raging hormones and increasing discomfort. He'd tried not to pressure her into sex although, God knows, if he had to smile through gritted teeth once more instead of tearing her clothes off he'd go mad. He'd tried to keep busy and show how much he really wanted the baby, how excited he felt at the idea of bringing up a family together. He'd already made a start on redesigning the garden – there would be a sandpit and a climbing frame. He had even been looking at school league tables one evening, although it had been hard to focus once Min had emerged from the shower, her swollen breasts burgeoning out of her robe. He knew she was feeling self-conscious at her changing and expanding body – she'd always had a thing about her weight on account of being just shy of five foot tall – so he made an effort not to focus on the bump, although he had taken every opportunity to stare at it in wonder and awe when she fell asleep, which was quite often, these days.

CHAPTER 12

OVER THE NEXT COUPLE of weeks Judy worked through a list that she kept folded in her makeup bag. It wasn't exactly a secret because Oliver could see most of the results when he returned home every evening, but it seemed too cruel to herald the actions in writing. Besides, words like 'ecdysis' sounded as if they needed natural yogurt next to them rather than indecently triumphant ticks.

Two mutually exclusive scenarios battled in her mind: how to leave and how to spare Oliver the pain he was going through. It sometimes seemed as though it would be easy to put a halt to any thoughts of going and to submit to what was, by anyone's standards, a comfortable life. He would forgive her – it wasn't too late.

Oliver arrived home upbeat every night, dying inside. He bought expensive flowers, embellished stories from the day at work, forced her to laugh by leaving little gaps in all the right places, kept his hands to himself in bed. One night, as she snored, he surveyed her tangle of hair, the curve of her neck and her bare shoulder, and began to sob silently as his pointless erection deflated. He gulped at the lack of middle ground available to him – he could cry quietly and eventually fall asleep or he could jump up, scream and rage and ... There was nothing in between.

As Judy handed over two bin bags of clothes in Oxfam on a chilly Friday afternoon, the woman behind the counter thanked her before making a strange sound – a nasal sussuration of understanding. A sisterly bonding over sludgy neutrals and once-comfortable shoes.

'Do you think I'm a cliché?'

'Do you think I'm a loser?'

'Supporting your pregnant partner isn't what losers do.'

'Unless they're pregnant by their dealer.'

Judy and Paul sat on high, uncomfortable stools in Café Italia, watching a group of beauty-therapy students negotiate the wet cobblestones.

'You don't know that for sure.'

'No, you're right. It could be any number of men, but I don't like to consider the entire list as it puts me off my lunch, Jude.'

They twirled spaghetti in unison.

'What does the doctor say?'

'Well, she thinks it's the dealer's because it looked like a menacing little bugger on the scan. You know, hunched over and all fists. They're doing some more tests.'

'Is she at her parents'?'

'Yep. Probably getting waited on hand and foot by Malty or whatever her name is.'

'Malty?'

'Used to be the nanny, then was the housekeeper and now she's just part of the fixtures and fittings. Lives in the grounds and is probably on a bigger salary than me.'

'You've never mentioned Malty before. Jesus! Who has a housekeeper?'

'She's not a housekeeper any more. And, anyway, Jen wanted to keep it quiet. It wasn't very "street" to have a Malty.'

'A housekeeper! Christ! Ooh, I'd have loved a Malty when I was a kid. My mum's idea of keeping us occupied on rainy weekends was to shove us in the spare room with a packet of Party Rings and the dressing-up box. There's only so much you can do with a feather boa, a couple of sun hats and the best bits of your dead nan's wardrobe.'

Judy smiled at the waitress and pointed to her glass for more Pellegrino.

'I'd love a Malty now,' he said. 'Someone at home, thinking about what to cook for me as she irons the pillowcases. Someone thinking about what I might want to wear tomorrow, and making sure it's not lying on the bedroom floor with spiders lurking in it.'

'Hmm. Cleaning the windows, folding my jumpers into squares, baking stuff – brownies, Victoria Sandwich cake ...'

'Jen doesn't even know how to use the washer.'

'Probably best that she's down with her family for now, though. She needs looking after until she decides what to do.'

'Oliver thinks *you* need looking after.'

Judy's fork stopped in mid-air. 'What?'

'We were a bit drunk.'

'What else did he say?'

The waitress placed the bottle of water on the table and retreated quickly.

'Nothing. Not much. I can't remember.'

'What else did he say, Paul?'

Her steadiness wobbled him.

'He talked about that retreat you went on. He said you were acting rather ...'

She was aware that he was building up to the important bit, trying to gauge how little would satisfy her, wondering if he'd have to go all the way. She would make him go all the way. Surely he understood her well enough to know that. They watched each other like sibling kittens: she was waiting to pounce; he was hoping she'd back off.

'He said that he thought you both needed a break – you know, a holiday together. He said you were thinking about going to Ibiza to buy another painting from Hannah what's-her-name, which might be a bit tricky because I hear she's at death's door after shoving too much crap up her nose.'

Judy narrowed her eyes, claws still out, resisting the temptation to be drawn into gossip. Hannah never had known when to stop.

'He says you've been very distant. He thinks you're having some sort of a …'

'What?'

'You know …'

'No! Jesus, Paul! What?'

'Nervous breakdown.'

Oliver was wrong on two counts. One: the term 'nervous breakdown' had gone out with floral aprons, back-street abortions and perms – the modern urbanite's fate is more likely to be an acute mental episode or a depressive collapse. And, two, Judy wasn't having any of the above.

Am I happy? What does that mean? Is this what I want? How can I answer that question if I don't know – can't know – the alternative? If I left, would Oliver wait in case I came to realize I'd made a mistake? Could I ever come back? Babies would have made me stay. Perhaps we should have had kids. Perhaps the abortion was the start of everything going wrong. Maybe I chose the wrong tine in the fork in the road. But we were kids ourselves. We weren't ready; I wasn't ready. I can't ever imagine being ready. Oliver cried like a baby himself the night before, sobbing into a towel in the bathroom so I wouldn't hear. I could have cancelled the appointment. I nearly did. He or she would be eleven now. Nearly ready for big school. Primary education, crayons, stickers, plastic lunchboxes, stabilizers, small plates all consigned to the past. Standing at the edge of sex, swearing, embarrassment, hormones, armpits, exams. I wouldn't have been able to leave a kid – and perhaps we'd have had more than one by now – to steer through that lot with only Oli for guidance. But there is no kid.

CHAPTER 13

I T WAS A SOURCE of much amusement to Judy's friends that she had a life coach. These strange gurus were, surely, the preserve of high-flying, high-blood-pressured executives. In fairness, Judy would never have sought one out, but she'd met Patrick at a party, liked him, liked the idea of being a bit more like him – seemingly sorted and utterly chilled – and had taken him up on his offer of a free session. She had no truck with the idea that talking over problems could magnify their significance and make them seem worse. And, anyway, she didn't always take problems to Patrick. Usually, she talked about what was going on in her life. Occasionally, they would plan ahead, using flip-chart paper and coloured pens. At the beginning, she had not told the whole truth. She had not said that sometimes she pretended to be asleep when she was awake, and pretended to be awake when she was asleep.

Over the past few months, she had been able to say things to Patrick that she had never, and probably would never, say to anyone else. She had planted seeds, trawled up sediment, wobbled. Sometimes she was surprised to see the same woman in the mirror afterwards.

She liked the first minute of those sessions more than the other fifty-nine, but she liked that minute so much that she felt like the rest of the hour was a fair price to pay. The minute started once Judy pressed the doorbell. There was no sound. Patrick either heard the click of the button or the bell rang in a room far enough away for it not to be audible outside. Somehow, he arrived at the door silently. He would then open it wide so that it touched the wall. He was always smiling as the door opened. Once it was open, he would say her name, just her name, nothing else, step to the side and wave her in with a slow half-sweep of his arm. Judy would say hello and walk past him along the hall into his coaching room. He would close the door behind them, usually as she released her bag on to the floor. She would remove her coat, which he would always take from her in a seamless and perfectly timed action, carefully placing it on a wooden hanger before placing it on the coat hook on the back of the door. As he did this, Judy would sink into the armchair, adjusting the cushions for optimum comfort, take a deep breath, and look out of the window at the ramshackle garden where herbs grew in chipped coffee mugs and old pans. Patrick would then sit down and wait for her to speak first. It was, in many ways, like the kind of dance couples tend to do when their song comes on – familiar and easy.

'I'm sorry I haven't been able to come for a while.' Judy knew he needed no explanation, but she wanted to set a context for what she was about to say for herself as much as for him. 'I know you can't tell me what to do, but I feel like I could do with …'

Without taking his eyes off her, Patrick poured tap water into two glasses. Judy paused and watched a ginger tom cat wash himself in a slice of sunlight. She felt the luxury of knowing she could take her time. She had found these silences very difficult at first, but now reclined into them as though they were warm baths that had been specially drawn and scented for her. The cat paused mid-lick, twitched his ears, rolled on to his left side, then back to his right, and closed his eyes.

'Just lately I've been having these daydreams where I can see Gina's face, from when we were little girls, you know?'

He nodded.

'And I can see all the life draining out of it, and everything goes quiet and still. And then I can hear things I don't normally hear. The wasps' nest at the bottom of the garden. Little baby birds crying for food. Like a sort of hyper-real …'

Patrick shifted in his chair, breaking the spell.

'Do you think I'm mad?'

'No.'

She realized she would have to rein it in, even with Patrick. Even in this chair where the words normally spilled out without censure.

'I know I should be grateful that everything turned out OK, but what's really happened is that it's made me think. It's made me think …' Judy was struck by the possibility that if she said anything that sounded like a clichéd coaching client, she might turn Patrick into a clichéd coach and lose the real him for ever. 'Oliver thinks I'm having a breakdown of some sort.'

Patrick stayed silent.

'I hate what this is doing to him – what I'm doing to him. It's killing us both.'

He took a sip of water, mainly to give her more time without feeling she had to speak.

Then it was as if she had been saving up all the words in a large trunk, had just managed to unfasten the tricky lock and flip open the lid. She explained how, a week ago, on the first day of December, after many heated and intense discussions, she had decided to move out of their shared bed but stay in the same house as Oliver until after Christmas. At one point, Patrick questioned her motivation for staying in the marital home, but all she could think of in response was that there was a lot to do over the festive season, and Oliver wouldn't manage it without her. She'd listed the annual chores on her fingers. Her right index finger extended as she described how to buy the right tree; her middle finger extended as she explained how carefully she stored the baubles and how each had a special place on the tree. On she went until all her fingers and both thumbs were spread in mid-air. With both hands raised like that, she looked as if she had a gun pointing at her.

Chapter 14

www.helpingyouthroughdivorce.com

Having a conversation with your spouse may help you to understand what is going wrong in the relationship. Raising your voice or making accusations is unlikely to bring out the best in either of you and may escalate bad feeling. It is advisable to start any discussion with a calm tone of voice. You might wish to rehearse a calm speaking voice and some key phrases in a private place where you will not be disturbed. Key phrases are the points you wish to get across – be careful not make your key phrases accusatory. 'I feel …' is better than 'You make me feel …' You should also avoid 'always' and 'never'. As it can be difficult to know exactly how your spouse will react, be aware that rehearsing key phrases can have its limitations. To speak to a divorce coach, click here and someone will get back to you within 24 hours.

***

'Where's your wedding ring?'

Oliver had walked into the kitchen without a sound.

Judy hastily closed her laptop and rubbed the fiercely pink groove in her fourth finger with the thumb and forefinger of her right hand.

'You've actually taken your ring off?'

'I just thought that …' She trailed off. She was tired and wasn't up for another argument.

'So everybody knows?' His voice was getting louder and higher. He was revving up for a big one.

'It depends what you mean by everybody, Ol. People aren't really interested in whether I'm wearing my ring or not. I don't think anyone's noticed, to be honest.'

'When did you take it off?'

'In the shower last night. It almost slipped off, so I thought I might as well put it somewhere for safe keeping,' she lied. In truth, she had gouged at it with soap, twisting and pulling at it until it had finally come off with a jerk. She had stamped her bare foot on it to stop it spinning down the drain.

'The safest place for it, Jude, is on your finger. That's why the vicar tells you to put it there.'

'That's if you're staying married.'

Oliver snatched Judy's cardigan clean off her shoulders, like a man reclaiming a stolen garment. She was part bemused, part alarmed, and offered limited resistance. She was feeling rather hot anyway. Bare-armed, with a dangling thread of wool hanging from her watch, she looked at her crazed husband and enquired as to what the fuck he thought he was doing. He threw the cardigan to the floor and grabbed her car keys off the kitchen table, desperate and wild-eyed.

'You're going nowhere!' He balled the keys into his fist.

'That's my point, Oliver. I'm going nowhere.'

'I mean you're not leaving this house!'

'That's ridiculous. What are you going to do? Tie me up?'

He considered it for a moment. Tying her up would be going too far but he could make things very difficult. 'I can make things very difficult, Jude. Don't fucking push me.'

'Oliver … Oliver …' She took his hands and sat him down on a dining chair. She scraped another chair out for herself. He wasn't sure if she was changing her mind – she'd certainly softened when she took his hands – or if she was about to try to convince him that this stupid idea of hers was the right thing for all concerned.

'Oliver, honey. Please. I have to leave. Trust me, it's the right thing in the long term.'

'Oh, yes! I'll thank you for leaving me in the end, I'm sure!'

'I'm not just leaving you. I'm leaving everything.'

'Are you trying to tell me this is nothing personal?' He started to stand up, but she lightly pushed him down into his seat; his stomach felt like a slightly deflated balloon under her taut palm.

'It's *not* personal. I know that sounds ridiculous but—'

'Fucking right, it sounds ridiculous! How can it be nothing personal? You're leaving me! On what grounds? If it's nothing personal, you have no grounds.'

'Can you stop being a lawyer for a moment?'

'And can you stop being a fucking idiot and look at what you're throwing away?' He spread his arms out to indicate himself and all that surrounded him: the Bosch oven, the Ikea kitchen, the beautiful oak floorboards, lovingly restored, and, out of the window, the maturing garden with apple trees – almost an orchard, they had once joked – and carefully tended borders. 'Is that what you want, Jude? To throw all this away?'

'I don't want to throw it away, Ol. I want to leave. I want to do something else with my life.'

'What? What do you want to do that you can't do here?'

'I have to get away. I don't know what I'm going to do yet, but I just know that I have to leave.'

'Oh, Christ! Is this your mate talking?'

'What?'

'Fucking Fruit Loops – Harry, or whatever idiotic name she's called.'

'It's nothing to do with Harry.'

'Is it Patrick, then?'

'No, Oliver! No! It's me!'

'You've changed.' He was sneering now, and she could see he would soon cry. 'You've *really* changed. Look at you. You've become a right cold-hearted bitch. You don't give a shit for anyone else's feelings. You sit there in your little bubble and plan to skip off to fuck knows where because, ooh, you're a bit bloody bored. Well, we're *all* fucking bored, Judy!' He was shouting in her face now. She could smell wine on his breath and a day's work on his shirt.

'I do give a shit. I don't want to hurt you, Oliver, but—'

'Oh!' He stood up fast and his chair toppled backwards on to the floor. 'Oh! She doesn't want to hurt me! Well, I'm sorry if I'm a bit hurt by my boring, BORING life crashing around my ankles!' He threw the fruit bowl at the wall. The shattering glass caused Judy to jump up. Her immediate instinct was to pick up the glass and the fruit, but she fought against it and sat down again.

Oliver rubbed his face with his palms, spreading fresh tears and snot all over his face, then furiously ran his fingers through his hair. He looked strikingly unhinged.

'Look – remember when my mum had that episode a few years ago, just after she retired?'

Judy didn't know where this was going, but he'd stopped shouting so she decided to hear him out. 'Yes?'

'Well, do you remember what happened?'

'What do you mean?'

'The doctor gave her some pills, Dad took her on holiday, they redecorated the living room and got a new conservatory. Do you remember?'

'Yes.'

'Well, then . . .'

'Sorry?'

'Let's get you to the doctor. I'll book some time off and we can think about that extension we've always wanted. You could have it as a music room! Or we can move. Fuck it! Yes! We'll move! Hey?'

'Oh, Oliver, it's not about moving.'

'We can do whatever you want!'

'I want to—'

'You could give up work! Hey? Give up work completely! I earn enough to support us, and we can—'

'Stop! Oliver, please stop! Please!'

They were both crying now.

'Please. This isn't going to be sorted out by a fortnight's holiday and getting the builders in.'

'No, you're not listening, Jude! Forget the extension! We can move!'

'It won't be solved by moving, either.'

'Then why are you moving out? If it won't be solved by moving, why are you doing just that?'

She was never going to win in this kitchen courtroom. She put the kettle on and started to make tea. 'Do you want a cup?'

'I want you to stay.'

'I CAN'T!' Her feet lifted off the ground as she screamed the words.

The phone rang. Oliver leaped for it.

'Hello? Oh, hello, Barbara . . . Yes, I'm on top form, thanks to Judy . . . What? . . . Oh, has she not talked to you about this idea she's had? . . . No? Oh, she's thinking of leaving, Barbara. Did you not know? . . . Yes, she has this idea that she can make a better life for herself elsewhere . . . Sorry? . . . I'm afraid I don't, Barbara, you'd have to ask her yourself . . . Yes, I think there is . . . Well, that's the funny thing, Barbara, it's not a man at all. No . . . Another woman . . . Yes . . . Oh, didn't you?'

'Give me the phone, you stupid sod!'

'Sorry, Barbara, she's asking to speak to you. I expect she'll be able to explain it better than I can because, to be honest, Barbara, I don't know what the hell is going on in my own home these days. 'Bye, Barbara. Nice talking to you.'

He thrust the phone at her. It grazed her cheekbone.

'Hello, Mum . . . Calm down! . . . No . . . No . . . Oh, for God's sake, no! . . . Yes . . . I don't know.'

'Hey!' Oliver shouted. 'Don't forget to tell her why she hasn't got those grandchildren she wants, will you, Jude? Don't forget! Because if you forget, I'll tell her! I'll be telling everyone everything, so you needn't think you're going to come out of this smelling of roses, sweetheart!'

He stormed out like a tantrumming toddler. Judy started to pick up the larger curls of glass with her free hand.

'Mum, if you'd just calm down for a minute, I can explain.'

Blood glooped from her thumb pad. She hadn't felt the glass pierce her skin but the evidence was now making the already grim domestic scene look as if it should be taped off and guarded by a uniformed officer.

'I don't know what he meant by that. He's just very angry and upset.'

Judy trapped the phone between her ear and shoulder, looking every inch the osteopath's nightmare, as she used her phone hand to wrap kitchen roll around her thumb.

'Mum. Mum. Mum, can you please just—'

The sound of Oliver thundering back downstairs made the people next door pause with their forks mid-air.

'Have you told her? Have you told her?'

She cradled the mouthpiece and glared at him.

'Do you want me to tell her?' He grabbed at the phone. 'I'll tell her! Give me the phone! I want her to know what her precious daughter is capable of!'

He wrangled it from her and swung out his arm to bat her away. She fell to the floor on the glass. Now she felt the shards. She brought her glassy hand up to her mouth, to stifle the sound of the shock, to protect her mum.

She tasted blood.

Now she could leave him.

CHAPTER 15

CHILLY SILENCES FEEL LIKE the dropped stitches of relationships. When you hold everything up to the light, there are little bullet holes.

Judy knew that Oliver could hear the carol singers making their way to their front door just by watching how his shoulders became more rigid with each turned page of his newspaper. As neither wanted to show they were getting any pleasure from anything at all, these days, the house had been silent of music and entertainment. Even the kitchen radio was switched off at six thirty p.m. sharp just in case either of them was tricked into laughing. Hence, the carol singers' progress could be heard from several doors along the street. By the time they reached next door, 'Once In Royal David's City' was wearing a bit thin and the vicar's voice had become as grating as a child's first attempt with a violin. They each realized that one of them would have to go to the front door, smile, listen to a bit of a carol, say something nice, then give them some cash and perhaps something festive, like a bag of chocolate coins. There was no mulled wine or mince pies this year.

Oliver decided it would be Judy's responsibility to see to the singers and, more importantly, to face the vicar, as she didn't seem to be doing very much – scribbling more idiotic ramblings into her stupid journal by the look of things – and he was reading about third-world debt. The moral high ground was a familiar place to him now, often followed by a plunge to the depths of despair. He didn't move as the doorbell chimed.

Judy handed a five-pound note to the vicar and gave each child a bag of chocolate coins. She apologized for the lack of mulled wine and mince pies this year.

'Well, I've had quite a bit of it this evening, so perhaps it's as well,' said the vicar. She fantasized that his hand on her shoulder was his way of telling her he understood what she was doing and that God was on her side, but she knew, deep down, that everybody else's mulled wine was taking its toll on his balance. Once she closed the door, she wiped the smile off her face and returned to the living room to hear the carollers strike up again next door. She couldn't face another half-hour of hearing them fade into the distance, so she retreated to the kitchen to clatter some dishes.

They hadn't discussed their plans for Christmas Day. The annual rolling schedule meant that they were duty-bound to spend it at Judy's parents and go to Oliver's parents for Boxing Day. Next year, they'd have swapped again: Oliver's parents for

Christmas Day and Judy's for Boxing Day. And the year after, they'd swap again. And so it would go on, until a parent died, which would be the point at which Judy and Oliver would open their doors to both families for Christmas Day, and Boxing Day would be spent at the home of the one remaining live parent. And if Judy hadn't gone and spoiled it, she and Oliver would now be looking forward to pulling crackers, eating too many roast potatoes and snoozing through the Queen's speech. Instead, there was a snowy hush.

Judy woke up on Christmas morning and thought about how this would be the last Christmas morning that she would wake up in her own spare room. This would be the last Christmas morning that her first bodily function would be to cry instead of pee.

Oliver opened her bedroom door like the new gunslinger in town.

'What the fuck?'

'Merry Christmas, Jude! Look at us! Waking up on Christmas morning in separate beds. No truce for Christmas?'

'What?'

'No truce?'

'Oliver, can we just get through this? Please? Can I just ask you to please think of my dad today?'

'Oh, a bit of goodwill – is that what you want? Yes, I can do goodwill, Jude.' He walked over towards her bed.

Judy pulled the duvet around herself. 'Get out,' she said.

He paused to consider if it was worth pushing his luck. He'd always loved how she looked before she'd arranged herself for everyone else's eyes. He loved seeing her off-guard and natural, all Betty Blue hair and traces of last night's eyeliner coagulated with crusty sleep.

'Do you remember that game we used to play, Jude? That yes-no game?'

'I mean it. Get out.'

'We did it on honeymoon – do you remember?'

She searched his face, wondering what was coming next.

'I'd ask you if ...'

'Please, Oliver, no . . .'

'No? Only it was all yeses back then, wasn't it? Even if it hurt a little bit – even when—'

'Oliver. Please. Please.'

'Yes, you used to say that, too. Please, Oliver. Please. Do you remember?'

She got out of bed, fronted up to him naked. 'Yes, I remember. Now can you please leave me alone?'

She had broken the spell. He stopped the serial-killer act. 'I'm going.' He moved towards the door, then turned back with a panto-style double-take. 'Oh, no! It's *you* who's going, isn't it? It's not me. It's you!' And he laughed a B-movie cackle all the way down the stairs.

Ten minutes later, she followed him. 'Oliver, can I ask you, please, to hold it together for today? Just for one last day?'

'Can I ask *you*, Judy, if you would *please* put some fucking clothes on? Do you think I want to see you flaunting yourself around like that? Are you *trying* to start something with me?'

Judy clawed the neck of her bathrobe closed and looked down. The robe reached all the way to her feet. 'What are you on about?'

'If you're going to swan around this place looking like that ...'

The phrase hung in the air.

'I'm going to make some breakfast.'

'Do what you like, Jude,' he growled. 'Happy Christmas!' He kicked a pile of books over with his bare foot.

Oliver barely recognized himself. He'd turned into the type of man he hated defending in court. Now he was against the ropes, his true colours were coming out.

His final half-hearted punch at his opponent took the form of driving too fast on the icy roads and cobbled streets to her parents' house. Judy stared out of the passenger-seat window, allowing tears to roll and drop, refusing to give him the satisfaction of knowing how much pain she was in.

Barbara and Ray had been up since six a.m. Barbara had been glad of the early start because there were potatoes and sprouts to be peeled, a turkey to be roasted and a hundred and one other jobs to do before Rob, Min, Judy and Oliver arrived. Ray was awake because he'd been sleeping odd hours – a nap here, a snooze there. As she stirred awake, Barbara had nestled under his arm and rested her head on his chest, the way she had always done. She had closed her eyes and imagined – wished – that things were like they used to be when Ray was well and Judy loved Oliver. She had kissed her husband's soft belly and burrowed down further. And, for half an hour, they had kept the world and its troubles at bay in the near-darkness of their marital bed. As Barbara later pulled on the clothes that she would worry and fret in all day, she promised herself a silk slip from the January sales.

Rob and Min arrived at noon and settled on the sofa, allowing Barbara to be mother. She poured cava and orange juice, placed little plates of canapés on occasional tables, beamed and listened as Min told dull stories of antenatal appointments, swollen fingers and her weight increase in kilos. Rob tried to convert kilos into stones and pounds for his parents. Ray sweated in his Christmas jumper, sang along to carols and occasionally joined in the conversation, levering in anecdotes from Barbara's pregnancies and Rob's adventures as a toddler. For an hour, they chatted and laughed. Barbara darted in and out of the kitchen, always returning to perch on the arm of Ray's chair. Min referred to her bump like a true first-time mum, almost constantly touching it, spanning her fingers across it, pressing her thumbs to feel for hands and feet, reaching for Rob's hand and putting hers over his as he felt for kicks. The chime of the doorbell was welcomed, not only because of who was on the doorstep but because the division of labour to keep the conversation alive and sparkling, as befits a Christmas Day, would be spread among a larger workforce.

'Hey, happy Christmas! It's Jude and Oliver!' Barbara threw her arms around the pair of them at once, accidentally banging their heads together.

'I just need the loo, Mum. Oliver, can you take the presents in, please?'

'Of course,' said Oliver.

'Hey, it's the man himself! Oliver! We've not seen you for a while with all your business trips to London, you flash bugger!' Ray wrapped his arms around his son-in-law, patting him on the back.

'Ha! Well, I'm here now! Happy Christmas! How are you?'

Ray rolled his eyes and jerked a thumb towards the kitchen, where his wife had returned to baste and worry. 'Well, the doghouse is shut for Christmas, so I should be fine.' He laughed.

Min bent over her bump to hug Oliver as Rob poured him a glass of supermarket cava.

'There you go, mate,' said Rob. 'Cheers and happy Christmas.'

Judy took a deep breath; it was going to be some afternoon.

Ray carved the turkey with all the expertise of a master butcher, then shoved each perfect slice into his own mouth as his family pretended not to notice and busied themselves with parsnips and an overfilled gravy boat.

'Parsnips, Dad?' asked Judy.

'I'm full, thanks,' he said, as he sat down still holding the large serrated knife, no longer interested in the meat or the meal.

Rob gently took the knife from him. He would now be on carving duty until the day Min glanced at their son in the way Barbara had glanced at him moments earlier.

'Tuck in, everyone!' trilled Barbara. 'I hope it's all right. I think the sprouts might be a little overdone, but better over than under with Brussels, I think.'

'It's lovely, Mum,' said Judy, 'and the roasties are gorgeous.'

'Goose fat. That's my secret ingredient! Just call me Nigella! I've even hidden coins, although someone's going to get a pound because I ran out of twenty-pence pieces.'

Min set down her cutlery and shot a sideways glance at Rob before making a tentative enquiry to anyone who would be able to answer the question: 'There are coins in the roast potatoes?'

'No, darling, the pudding!' giggled Barbara. 'And I'm setting fire to it! Vodka!'

The meal was clearly lacking the excitement of a naked flame.

'Do we need the actual fire, Mum?' asked Judy, glancing at Rob who was, by now, getting a bit fed up with catching and interpreting all these glances.

'I'm doing *everything* Nigella's way this year. I've even been sipping a glass of wine while I was doing the veg. I think that's how I've let the sprouts go, to be honest.'

'It's all lovely, Mum,' said Rob, making a 'shut-up' face at his sister.

The cracker pulling, as usual, sent the cat screaming out of the room. Everyone wore their paper hats and plastic rings, read out their jokes and riddles and blew festive tunes on whistles and kazoos. The flaming pudding didn't happen; Barbara only remembered after she had blobbed cream on to it. A bulb on the tree flickered and went out. A couple of baubles dropped off, taking a shower of pine needles with them. The poinsettia drooped a little; it had been Ray's job to water it that morning but he'd watered the Christmas tree instead. Everyone aahed at gifts they would recycle, return or put in the guest bathroom. The Queen frowned through another dreary speech.

Ray slept all the way through *Mamma Mia*.

Barbara rested her eyes when Pierce Brosnan started singing, and opened them again for the credits.

Min disappeared to the loo during every ad break and Rob took the opportunity to smile at his phone each time. He ate everything that was passed to him, dropping wrappers, tangerine peel and nut shells into a little pile at his feet.

Oliver made his way through Min's gold and frankincense chocolates and most of the bottle of champagne that Santa had kindly left for him.

Judy flicked through a couple of mediocre autobiographies that still had their half-price stickers attached.

At one point, Oliver laughed at something Rob said and rested his hand on Judy's knee. She flinched and looked at the hairy knuckles, as though a tarantula had crawled on to her. He withdrew it and glared at the television.

After the film, Judy escaped to wash the dishes. There was no dishwasher, nor would there ever be. It was a sponge scourer and Fairy Liquid for everything from the finest china to the biggest, clunkiest pans. Up to her elbows in suds – she'd forgotten how much to use and had been a bit enthusiastic with her squeeze – she looked out of the window at snow fit for Hollywood. She could see across the gardens into the Cardwells' house. The back door was open and they were putting on coats and scarves. Eight-year-old Celeste was first outside, balling snow into her little gloved hands ready to throw at her older brother, whose main aim of the day was clearly to move the carrot from their snowman's face to somewhere more amusing. Judy found herself giggling at it as she dried the last of the dishes.

'I think it's time we were leaving,' Oliver had walked in behind her. 'You'll have to drive,' he said, waving the almost empty champagne bottle.

CHAPTER 16

JANUARY. FEBRUARY. THOSE MONTHS flew past, although nobody was having fun. Judy decided to stay until the college could secure a permanent replacement for her, which gave her some thinking space about what she might do next.

'Where will you go?'

'Oliver isn't asking you to ask me stuff, is he, Paul?'

'I can't believe you're even saying that.'

The staffroom was empty apart from the two of them. They sat facing each other with their feet intertwined.

'Well, I don't know where I'm going and it's one of his favourite questions.'

'I'm asking because I'm genuinely interested. I mean, you could go anywhere.'

'I might come to Brazil with you. How would that be?'

'You'd be bored. It's a hundred per cent football this trip.'

'I could do other stuff while you're coaching the little boys who'll kick our little boys' arses in a few years' time.'

'You don't want to come to Brazil.'

'You don't want me to come to Brazil, you mean.'

It was true. He couldn't think of a single person he wanted to take with him. He wanted to arrive without baggage or expectation, light on his feet. He couldn't say so, of course.

'What time's your next lesson?' he asked.

'I might go to Edinburgh. Harry's said I can stay with her for a bit.'

'Right.'

'What?'

'Nothing. Edinburgh's nice.'

'But?'

'It's a bit of a hike. A long way to come round for a cup of tea.'

'So is Brazil.'

'I'm not thinking of living there.'

'Well, you can come and stay.'

Someone knocked on the door.

Paul leaned over Judy so that he could see who it was. His right cheek rested on Judy's left breast. It was accidental, but to move would seem odd, so he stayed in position, feeling the warmth on his cheek spread across his face. 'Yes, Chelsea?'

'Can I see you about this assignment, please, Paul?'

Almost all of Paul's female students needed extra help with their assignments.

'Sure.' He jumped to his feet and walked over to the door, cursing the telltale stirrings of an erection. 'See you later, Jude.'

She might go to Edinburgh. She wouldn't go to Brazil. At least her feet weren't quite so leaden when she walked around town, these days. She felt she might actually be able to jump on a train without suspecting the doors might close in front of her face, denying her access.

She'd felt a bit of bounce coming back, too. Bounce was something she had started to notice – in herself and others – after reading a magazine article ('Get your bounce back!') in which husbands who had had affairs were interviewed. Those featured in the piece had justified their actions by bemoaning a lack of bounce in their wives. These men, who might or might not have had bounce themselves – it was never discussed – charted their exes' progress through key perceived stages: from skipping girls ('I used to chase her around the playground!') to bouncy girlfriends ('Sometimes we'd just park the car in a country lay-by and clamber into the back seat!') to loving brides ('Our honeymoon was the best time of my life!') to dead-eyed wives ('She cared more about the dog than she did me!') and, finally, to bitter divorcees ('It's all about the money now – she's just out for what she can get!'). The men explained how they had been driven away from their spent spouses in search of more bounce, which they often conveniently found on dance floors less than half an hour from home. Low lighting, loud music, alcohol on tap, and bouncing women. Heaven.

Judy's slight bounce didn't go down so well with others. There were no joint invitations to anything, although there wasn't much going on in January or February anyway. Her mum wore her down with sighs and hugs and frequent murmurs of 'Oh, Judy'. Dad shook his head a lot, probably because he wasn't quite sure what was going on. Rob seemed to believe that taking her quietly to one side, usually in their parents' kitchen, and dispensing advice about how she might go about saving her marriage would make her reconsider her plans. He ended these ridiculous monologues by tapping his temple with a forefinger and telling her to 'think about it', as though she hadn't considered that. It was all she could do not to laugh.

Judy had dreaded Valentine's Day and had considered going away for the weekend, but she took to her bed and buried her nose in a book for the day. Paul cleverly invited Oliver over for dinner and they covered the neutral and upbeat territories of wine, wine holidays, British weather, football, Brazilian women and very keen trainee female lawyers.

Min went into labour at four p.m. on Valentine's Day, and gave birth to an eight-pound baby boy around midnight. Rob carried the engagement ring he'd planned to give her over dinner to the hospital, just in case the opportunity arose to go on bended knee. Funnily enough, it did not, and he forgot all about it until he put his trousers in the washing basket the next day and it rolled right out of his pocket and under the bed. He'd fish it out another time: it wasn't going anywhere, and he was beyond tired.

A week later, Jen miscarried her dealer's baby. She went through a full labour. Paul held her hand throughout – a gesture rooted more in humanity than love.

CHAPTER 17

THE PHONE RANG. OLIVER picked it up in the hope that it would be for Judy. Interaction – any interaction – would do.

'It's Harry for you.'

Harry and Judy had met up twice since the retreat and had spoken at least once a week. They were still in the first infatuated flush of friendship. They circled and bounced around each other, wholly and utterly present, with only selective narratives as proof of their pre-retreat existence. Two more notches of a dial and they'd have consumed each other.

Oliver despised this woman with a man's name, even though he'd never met her. Just the sound of her patronizing voice was enough to turn his mood foul. Because of fucking Harry, half his evenings were now soundtracked by his wife – yes, *his* wife – telling this bloody woman all about a few bars of music she'd written while he – *like a bloody mug* – had been out at work all day. And then it'd go quiet except for a few murmurs as she listened to what Harry had done with *her* day. Nobody asked *him*. Nobody wanted to know if *his* day had been fine.

His thoughts terrified him. The previous evening, he had heard Judy coughing in the kitchen. She had swallowed a tiny salmon bone. Within seconds, her coughing had turned into choking, and he had jumped up and run to her. For a moment – surely it was only a half-breath in terms of time – he had found it compelling to watch as she opened her mouth, rounded her shoulders and splayed her fingers. The synapses and muscles that would power his arm to hit her on the back felt strong enough to launch a space shuttle, and he hesitated. He wondered if he could dislodge what was choking her without relishing the opportunity.

Retch. At last! She coughed out the bone, and it splash-landed in its own little pool of vomit, barely making a sound. On all fours now, Judy took a deep breath and lifted her head.

And then they had stared into each other's eyes for longer than they'd done in months.

He had lost the opportunity to save her, paralysed by the raging heat of his anger. He would later reflect that, for more than a split second, he had wished her dead.

Judy knew she had to move out soon, but she had, just lately, secretly doubted that she would. Her life was relatively painless most days, and Oliver's belief that their marriage was not over was so firm, so fixed, that she wondered how she could hold on to an opposing view. Some days, when she had little by way of fight in her, she would pretend to herself that nothing had happened. Occasionally, she made bigger portions of stews and soups without immediately freezing or chilling the excess, and Oliver would silently reheat the leftovers and eat in front of the television. It was not an uncomfortable game they played on those days.

After checking that she was not physically attached to the house by a chain or a thread or obligated by some written deed, she had blamed her inertia on a sense of loyalty to the college. When Audrey had rushed up to her in the corridor last week to say they had found the ideal candidate for her job, she had tried to respond with an expression that said, 'I *am* glad. I hope he or she is just what you're looking for. I hope he or she will have faith in the students that drive everyone crazy. It's great news. Really. Now I can go. I can leave all of this behind. I'm so very glad.' Instead, she had given a little 'Oh!' that was too quiet for any human ear, even her own.

She hadn't *expected* their friends to rally around her, of course. The cancer scare was over and Oliver was now the injured party. There was never any question that the tsunami of sympathy would head his way. To be fair, he hadn't wanted it. His pain was acutely embarrassing to him, and he was mortified when others caught a glimpse of it. He'd only let Judy see it. He would hold it up to her shamelessly, shining beams of it into her eyes at two a.m. when he couldn't sleep and she didn't deserve to. She wanted to call Paul or Gina and tell them that *she* was in pain, that she couldn't remember a

109

day without hot tears and a screaming headache. She wanted to tell them about the night she'd found Oliver drunk and tugging on a belt he'd tied to the hall-light fitting, testing how much weight it would hold. How she had let him have sex with her on the stairs a few short weeks ago and had, afterwards, vomited pale green bile from the pit of her stomach. Some days, she'd have told them all of it in return for a pair of arms around her that wouldn't then try to snake under her top.

Packing was a vile ordeal. She had been thinning out drawers and cupboards for months, kidding herself that Oliver wouldn't notice. She'd used her parents' spare room for storage of her jewellery box, winter clothes and most precious books. And now she was packing in secret, like a teenage runaway, squirrelling and stuffing away the last of what she wanted. She mentally wrote off everything she was leaving, knowing that Oliver was more than capable of making a frenzied bonfire with the lot of it. The thought of him rifling through her underwear made her flesh creep, so she emptied those two drawers directly into a suitcase. She stuffed clothes into a rucksack, and a weekend bag bulged with shoes, toiletries and books. She lobbed everything into the boot of her car and resisted the temptation to drive off there and then. Over the course of the next few hours, she would open the boot to put in yet more belongings – a raincoat, a tangle of scarves, a pair of boots. All aboard the life raft.

She waited to face him. She wanted to give him the opportunity of calling her mad, unhinged, ungrateful, vindictive, a heartless bitch. She would leave with threats ringing in her ears and globs of wine in her hair that he'd thrown at her. It was the least she could do. It wasn't a selfless act, even though that was how she packaged it up for herself. She knew, on a subconscious level, that there was nothing quite like rancorous insults ringing in your ears and wine in your hair to make you realize you were driving towards a better place.

CHAPTER 18

IT IS A COMMON belief that the only people who gravitate away from sleepy, labyrinthine suburbs to live in shiny new cities are the super-creative, the high-flying, the innovative, the patent seekers and the big spenders: those who have outgrown their home town. It's not true. A million people each week arrive in the world's cities. Some are high-flyers, sure, but office juniors, nail technicians, bakers, plumbers and knife-wielding criminals are also among those who fancy their chances in a more bustling environment. Most arrive wide-eyed and squash their belongings into tiny bedsits and box rooms. They adjust to being smaller fish for a while, and spend evenings worrying over headlines that shout about rising knife crime in their neighbourhood. Some have a go at nonconformity for a while – perhaps buying unsuitable hats or taking up a habit they missed out on in their adolescence – until they make friends and start to fall in line again.

Social scientists are fascinated by our burgeoning cities and hypothesize that one can measure many things by population size, including how fast people walk. Small towns and villages are full of amblers and pausers, apparently, whereas cities are buzzing with people permanently on the verge of breaking into a trot. The faster-walking could, of course, be related to the rising knife crime but nobody had researched that particular correlation at the time of going to press. However, what has been established is that nearly everyone prefers a moderately complex environment; even idyllic sea views are more attractive to us if there's an odd boat or two bobbing around in universally appealing blue water. We're even happier if we're wondering why that boat is there – mystery is part of the visual and psychological allure.

Our preferred intensity of visual stimulation changes with our age and stage of life, and Judy had been operating with a low-to-medium level for some time, developing emotional cataracts, that reflected or perhaps even contributed to her general *ennui*. There had been rare exceptions, like when she'd managed to find time to draw and paint rather than sketch or scribble, or when she had wandered into her garden during the few hours that the sun shone on her riot of scarlet geraniums, lighting them up as if they were connected to the mains.

Judy unfolded herself out of the car after driving for 250 miles without a break, and breathed in cold, spring air. Edinburgh had a hoppy, toasty smell.

The Circle was the kind of café where you could rock up at eight a.m. and nurse one cappuccino after another from behind a dog-eared Penguin. Solid gold. Judy's appetite returned as soon as she glanced at the menu. Soon she was wolfing down double poached eggs (free range, from the happiest of hens) on thick white toasted doorsteps slathered with proper salted butter.

She had spent the night on her increasingly sagging sofa and had made an early dart just as the sun was rising, to avoid another portion of Oliver. The four-hour drive to Edinburgh reminded her of the time she and a college friend had had their drinks spiked. Nothing seemed real yet every sensation was heightened. She'd turned on the radio, for company more than anything, but had been disturbed by the sounds that had bounced sharply off the windows. The top left portion of her head had also been strangely compelling in the rear-view mirror. She needed a long, deep, dark sleep enveloped between tucked-in sheets.

She hadn't called Harry yet. She knew the offer to stay had been genuine, but she worried that Harry might not have fully thought it through – the hassle of getting spare keys cut and sharing a bathroom was only the start. One of Oliver's friends had stayed with them for three months a few years earlier, and they'd never seen him since. He had been a great guest – generous to a fault, buying wine every night and more at the weekend, cooking special meals made from organic ingredients he'd sourced at the market, insisting on washing up encrusted pans and the finest stemware. But in the end he became the embodiment of too-much-of-a-good-thing. Judy had found herself longing for the kind of evening in which an inadvertently empty fridge had meant Jacob's Cream Crackers and wrinkly apples for tea.

'Shall I take that away?' Judy looked up into a sweet, smiling face. The waitress was wearing a floral apron that was far too big for her. Underneath, she had on a 1960s pea-green shift dress. Judy nodded and the girl whisked away a plate containing a tiny amount of toast crust and not a trace of egg yolk. She returned with a fresh cappuccino and winked as she took the old one away. She appeared seconds later with a pristine *Guardian*. Judy fought not to cry as she realized she was being looked after. She idled through the paper, sipping her coffee, but even Marina Hyde's pages couldn't lift her spirits this morning.

Where are you? Are you OK? Px

Ah, the real world. Paul's text made her stomach lurch at the thought of having to tell everyone that she'd done the unforgivable, the unfathomable, the indefensible.

Am in Edinburgh. Am OK. Have you spoken to Oliver?

Without waiting for a response, Judy stuffed her phone into her coat pocket and got up to pay. She managed a half-smile and a thank-you, but the waitress wasn't fooled and responded with a tight little smile of her own. She paused at the door and stared at the street. She knew that, once she stepped out, she needed to know which direction to walk in. She turned right.

He rang me about half an hour ago. He's devastated. Can u spk? Px

She could, technically, speak, but she had nothing to say that would make sense in response to the questions he'd ask. How did she feel? She didn't really know. Full of coffee, egg, toast and remorse, disoriented, free, guilty, stupid, tired. What were her plans? She had none.

She idled for a couple of minutes, reading cards in a newsagent's window. There was clearly no excuse for not doing yoga in Edinburgh – even on a Wednesday there were three classes. And if you wanted an Indian head massage, three people could oblige you. One was doing it on a buy-one-get-one-free offer, which was either a very good deal for most people or only fair for the polycephalous demographic.

The traffic was building up to a standstill and she walked in the opposite direction to most of it, along Inverleith Row, until she came to a hotel that had views of the tops of some of the trees in the Botanical Gardens. She checked in for two nights to give herself time to think about what to do next. As lovely as the view was, the sight of the huge bed was more pleasing to her. She locked the door, switched off her phone, climbed into the coolest, cleanest sheets she had felt for a while, and slept soundly for nine hours.

When she woke, it took her a moment to remember where she was. It was dark and quiet in the room although she could hear traffic outside. As she sat up, she heard a crockery-laden trolley being pushed along the corridor. She switched on the bedside light and looked at her watch. Eight fifteen p.m. She groaned as she thought of the parking ticket she'd now have on her windscreen – if they hadn't towed the car. She switched on her phone. As it sorted itself out, she went into the bathroom. She unwrapped the complimentary soap and idly wondered if anyone ever used the shoe-polish kit. She couldn't face the bigger thoughts. Her phone beeped. Four texts, three missed calls.

10.59: Going into class. Spk l8r. P x

13.02: Call me when you get this. P x

13.17: Hi Jude. You OK? Harry x

17.52: FFS Jude! Call me! Worried about you! Paul

She rang her voicemail.

'*You have three new messages. First message, sent today at thirteen fifty-nine:* "Hi, Jude, it's Harry. Can you give me a call? Speak soon. 'Bye!"

'*Second message, sent today at fifteen twenty-one:* "Jude, it's Paul. Hope you're OK. Can you call me, please?"

'Third message, sent today at seventeen forty-nine: "Jude, I'm really worried now. Please just call me or text to let me know you're OK."'

Before heading out to find her ticketed (perhaps towed) car, she texted Paul and Harry:

Sorry. Am OK. Am in hotel in Edinburgh. Slept all day. Will call you later. Love Jude X

Although she'd slept for a full nine hours, she had no more clarity about what she would say to Paul, Harry or anyone else. She knew that any conversation would eventually lead to the question of what she planned to do now, as if she'd been masterminding some great scheme all along and could move her finger down a list and read the next entry. She was lost, metaphorically and, as it turned out, literally. She circled the New Town squares and cobbled side streets for her car. Just before she gave up and resigned herself to the fact that it had been towed, she spotted it. The missing wing mirror (sheared off by a school-run mum) and curled-up parking ticket gave it the look of an abandoned vehicle that had been standing there for far longer than an afternoon and evening. As she fished in her bag for the keys, she made eye contact with a man at least ten years her junior. As he passed her, he nodded and smiled, which caused her involuntarily to arrange her features into the closest thing to an unforced smile she had expressed in quite some time.

She rang Harry from the car and agreed to meet her in some place called Henderson's in an hour. She quickly decided that she couldn't face hearing a voice from 'home' this evening, so texted Paul to say she was on her way out and would speak tomorrow.

Henderson's was a vegetarian restaurant in the way that Glastonbury is a gig. Judy was so spoilt for choice that she had to allow a group of people ahead of her while she craned at the specials board and peered over the bain-maries of gorgeousness. As she did this, Harry was hectoring in her left ear.

'There's no need to stay at a hotel when I have a spare room!'

'I'm fine at the hotel for now, and I'm booked in for a couple of nights anyway. I just need to have some time on my own to think.'

'But it'll cost you a fortune and I hate to think of you on your own!'

Why did people hate to think of other people on their own? What was so bad about being on your own for a short while?

'Harry, I *want* to be on my own for a bit. I want some peace. I have to think about what I'm going to do.'

'Well, when you're ready, my spare room's there for you,' she replied, before she pushed an eighth of a pizza into her mouth.

Judy found it easier not to think about what people thought of her leaving town, leaving Oliver, leaving her job, leaving her brother to cope with being a new parent, leaving Mum to cope with Dad's ongoing decline. Rob, however, wasn't about to let her off quite so lightly.

'Mum's been trying to get you for the past couple of days,' he said. 'She's worried about you, Jude, and she's got enough to worry about without that. Can you call her?'

'I *have* called her. There's nothing else to say. Tell her I'm OK.'

'Oh, yeah! That'll soothe her nerves. I'm caught in the middle here, Jude. I've got Mum at one side, fretting like mad, and a screaming baby in my other ear, while you're languishing in a bloody five-star hotel. Do you not think we're all going through enough having to deal with Dad?'

It wasn't five-star – far from it – and she wasn't languishing. The hotel was being refurbished before the summer rush and Judy had managed to negotiate a cheap deal to stay in the smallest guest room for a couple of weeks. The owners neglected to tell her that the hammering and sanding would wake her up every morning, and that she would fall asleep heady on paint fumes every night. Even so, it was a haven; shelter from the real world for a while.

She realized there was no way of making Rob (or her mum or Min) understand why she'd had to leave, but she knew they would continue to badger her for answers. She wanted people to retreat until she was ready to talk. Even Harry. She wanted people to rally around Oliver and make him better. She wanted to forget he'd tied a noose in a rope even though she now knew it had been no more than a Boy Scout exercise. She wanted the omnipresent thought that she'd completely fucked up to go away. She wanted to start afresh, to get rid of the clothes she had left. She wanted a bit of peace.

Some people, of course, were more than happy to back off. It was easy for them to fall short of understanding, to gossip and demonize. Even easier, if there was consensus between friends. And easier still if it formed part of the loyalty package offered to the wounded party in the situation. Oliver actually felt uncomfortable with his friends' sympathy. In all honesty, he didn't appreciate the wholesale criticism of Judy, either. It wasn't quite loyalty he felt for her; he couldn't put his finger on why his hackles rose when the people who had been their mutual friends blithely picked up their hatchets. He wished they would stop.

It wasn't only friends, but people whom Judy had previously met only at occasional functions, or colleagues of Oliver's they'd bumped into when milling around the shops on a Saturday afternoon. Through such minimal contact, these people had been able not only to form a fairly rounded opinion of Judy, but also saw fit to share it with Oliver. And then there were the divorcees who had heard it on the grapevine and who had been biding their time, waiting for their moment to pounce.

Paul had been the only one, as far as Oliver could make out, who hadn't taken up arms against Judy. Even so, when they talked, Oliver was aware that Paul was hearing two sides of everything, and often found himself making a case rather than having a conversation. There were some areas that, as drunk as they might get, he would never be able to broach with Paul. He left those to Judy. The suicide incident, for example. He'd never meant to commit suicide – he realized he didn't have it in him

– but he had wanted a physical manifestation of his pain, so he had made a noose. It had made sense at the time, tying that knot, sliding the rope back and forth. It had even made sense to put it around his neck, which he did, sitting there wearing it like a necklace, but he'd never have taken the final drop. He didn't know if Judy knew that. He secretly hoped she didn't. He wanted her to suffer quite a bit for now.

CHAPTER 19

Children deprived of love are tethered to happiness with thread as weak as old promises. They cease to thrive, they shrink and shrivel, snarling at teachers, baring their pain to anyone brave enough to look. Unloved girls try to make babies with unloved boys, who carry stolen kitchen knives and worse in their pockets. These children are empty. They are ticking bombs, and are statistically unlikely to be healed. They will slash their own arms or gorge themselves to carb-fuelled apathy or eat nothing and make us see their very bones. They will turn on each other, they will riot in the streets, and we will follow them with brooms, making nothing clean. Even children swaddled in love and warmth through the easy and the difficult years are not immune from the inevitability of feeling unloved; it comes to us all in various ways – fleetingly, gradually, suddenly, sometimes permanently. It stops us in our tracks and we snarl at our bosses and show our pain in post-midnight texts and emails. Unloved women deafened by empty, aching wombs find unloved, angry men who will make promises they cannot keep. Crying on the kitchen floor is the least of it.

Wednesday. There were three pressed shirts hanging in Oliver's wardrobe. One was a dinner shirt, but the other two could be worn to the office. He could hold everything together until Thursday close of business, but he'd need another shirt for Friday. He took a moment to consider if he could get away with wearing the dinner shirt to work on Friday and putting his entire laundry basket and the stuff off the bedroom floor into the dry cleaner's over the weekend. He sat on the edge of the bed and stared into the wardrobe at its smooth, white back, which had been incrementally revealed by an unprecedented shortage of ironed shirts and dry-cleaned suits. A dog barked in the distance.

His life felt post-apocalyptic. He had no idea of what lay ahead. Oliver had always been so sure of everything because, apart from the odd glitch, everything had happened in textbook order for him. Long trousers had followed short. He had gone from school to college to university in one long tumble of exams and revision. He'd taken a condom to the teenage party where he'd lost his virginity. His life was mapped, written in something fine and dark and indelible. He had been sure, absolutely sure, of his love for Judy and hers for him. They had been blissfully in love at the start, and that had developed over time to pragma, a quieter love, a sharing of dishwashing, birthday breakfasts in bed. And then a meteor had hit the earth.

He had hoped that when Judy finally left, almost a week ago, it might be a relief. But by trying to be kind, trying to soften the blow over interminable weeks, she'd effectively been pulling off his wings and then his legs, one by one, until he was left twisting and desperate.

Endless nights of serious talk had preceded her departure. Those conversations would start hesitantly, as though they didn't have a sea of shared language from fifteen years together on which to sail the words. Eventually, Oliver would start to massage his temples or Judy would cover her face with flat, closed palms. It had rattled Oliver that she continued to talk with her face covered in that way. He could barely make out what she was saying, but felt he would be adding to her distress by asking her to repeat herself. Maybe the secret was behind those hands. Maybe she had given him the answer to his question and he'd been too fucking polite to ask her to fucking well enunciate more clearly or to move her hands away from that gorgeous mouth of hers. But what could he have said? 'Sorry, Jude, what was that? No, not that bit. The bit after the bit where you intimated I was boring. The bit just before you suggested you'd been – correct me if I'm wrong – sleepwalking through your life, through our marriage.'

He couldn't decide if it was cruel or careless of her to leave stuff behind. He didn't dare hope it was because she might come back. What was he supposed to do with a box of Tampax, Lapsang Souchong tea bags or a CD of Take That's greatest hits?

He shuffled into the living room and tipped the Tampax on to the table where they scattered and rolled around. He unwrapped one, removed the tubing, wrapped the string around his forefinger, spun it around a bit, then threw it against the wall. He surveyed the chaos. He liked how the tampon looked on the carpet next to a take-away carton near an almost drained bottle of wine. It would fucking serve her right to see this now. It would serve her right to walk into this shithole and inhale, and for the stench to catch in her throat.

He rang Agnes to ask her to come and do an extra cleaning shift.

Oliver wasn't very good at grocery shopping. He found this quite astonishing at first because it was his understanding, almost to the point of it being a fact, that he'd been able to do it well enough when Judy had been around. However, he now saw that he'd probably contributed only snacks and trolley-pushing power to their weekly grocery trip. As he shuffled around the aisles of the supermarket, he wondered whether he should come up with a system for keeping the cupboards stocked with things he didn't think about but definitely needed: salt, laundry liquid, toilet rolls and the like.

'Oh, hi, Oliver!'

Steph Lewis had been stalking her prey for long enough to alert the attention of the security guard and his colleagues, watching the CCTV footage from the comfort of their office.

'Steph. Hi, hi. How are you? Sorry, I'm just stocking up. Just wondering if I have enough salt. Ha! Dear me. How are you? You look well.'

She looked like a woman who had spent an awfully long time in front of a mirror.

'I'm fine, Oliver. I was so sorry to hear about you and Judy.'

'Yes, well, yes. These things happen. I, erm …' He scratched his head and wondered how he could get away without actually running.

'You're not actually *eating* that, are you?' Steph picked up a microwave dinner from his trolley and tipped the side with the ingredients list towards her. 'Good God, Oliver, it's full of all kinds of rubbish!' She touched his arm, and he flinched.

'Well, it's more for convenience, really. I'm so busy at the office and by the time I get in …'

'Oh, no. Oliver, honestly, this stuff will be the death of you. Please. I'm going to take this from you and put it back. I'm going to make you something proper and you and I can sit down with a nice bottle of wine—'

'Oh, no. No, really …' His mind flitted to a documentary he'd watched the previous night about recent scientific developments in the manufacture of invisibility cloaks.

'No! Oliver, I won't hear of it. You and I can sit down over a nice bit of salmon and some sautéed potatoes and a glass of something chilled, and you can tell me what to do about my neighbour's plum tree that's creeping over into my garden. I need a man of the law to tell me what to do. A bit of professional advice? What do you say?'

'You really would need to look at your deeds, Steph. I don't actually specialize in that kind of thing and—'

'No excuses! I'm cooking you dinner. Let's say next Tuesday. How does that sound? Tuesday. You can't be doing anything on a Tuesday. Nobody does anything on a Tuesday. So Tuesday? Yes?'

It was no use. She wouldn't accept a no. He considered saying yes and making an excuse on the day, but that would delay the inevitable.

'OK, that'll be lovely.'

'Right. Now, shall I come to you and cook or do you want to come to me?'

Christ almighty. 'No, no, no … I'll come to you. Around eight, if that's all right?'

'Fabulous! Now can you remember where I am? I'm at twenty-three—'

'Yes, yes. That's fine. I know where you are. Just near the bus stop.'

'That's right.' She smiled. 'Now, no more of this horrible nonsense.' She held the boxed meal as if it was a soiled nappy. 'I'm going to put this naughtiness back on the shelf.' And off she went, giving him the kind of twee wave that told him she would definitely have soft toys on her bed.

Steph swept the soft toys off her pink satin duvet in one meaty move, displaying all the strength and dexterity of a woman who hadn't had sex in five and a half months. She'd ambushed Oliver on his way out of the en-suite bathroom, kissing him as he turned off the bedroom light. The whirring and rattling of the bathroom extractor fan proved a rather off-putting soundtrack to their fumblings, and Oliver wondered aloud if it might be an idea to switch it off.

'I like it with the lights on, Oliver. Don't be shy now.'

'No, I was just thinking of the electricity. That fan uses a lot. If you switched it off …'

'Bugger the fan. Now if you just kick off those shoes, I can get these down …' She bit his cheek and tugged at his trousers, inadvertently scratching his thighs with her alarming fingernails.

'Steph, I think you're lovely, I really do, but I'm not sure …'

She clenched her jaw and stood up, tilting her head back in a subconscious display of dominance. In the bathroom glare, she looked rather fearsome, he thought. She took a deep breath, marched to the bathroom, switched off the fan and returned to the bedroom. She removed her skirt and unbuttoned her blouse in what she thought was an alluring way. Her features were softened now, lambent with the sodium glow of the street light through the pale unlined curtains. A bus rolled by and the top deck illuminated her further, brightening her shoulders and clavicle. She had a swimmer's torso. It occurred to him that he'd seen her swim once. She'd been fast, sleeking through the water, leaving everyone else in her trail. She had even won something or other, hadn't she? It had been in the local paper. He vaguely remembered the picture of the mayor in full regalia shaking the hand of a shivering swimsuited adolescent.

'OK. Are we all right now, darling? The light's off, the fan's off.'

'Didn't you once swim? Competitively, I mean?'

'Yes. I did. I swam for Lancashire. Now, Oliver, that was a long time ago. Let's get back in the here and now, hey? Let's start with a bit of breast stroke, shall we?'

It was a horrible little invitation that he could tell she had used before. However, he knew when he was defeated and pushed his shoes off. He closed his eyes, breathed in airport-bought perfume, and thought of the medal shining against Steph's once proud chest.

The more Oliver's life spiralled into freefall, the more women seemed to magic themselves up at various locations. Steph and her salmon were only the start of things. Nowhere was safe. Even one of the clerks at work had taken to sending him recipes and film reviews. She would follow up each email with casual-sounding conversations in the corridors and on the stairs. She'd appear seemingly from nowhere, more often than not startling him into making an involuntary whimper, and would catch him by the arm: 'Oh, that film is on this weekend if you fancy catching it,' or 'If you need any help with that recipe, let me know, because I think I've found a better way of doing it.' Oliver would smile and mutter a vague response along the lines of getting back to her. He was absolutely amazed at the effect of being abandoned by one's wife. He felt like he'd discovered a big secret: this was the way to attract women – all you had to do was get one to leave you. How hard could that be?

Shaking off Steph proved a little troublesome. She turned up at his office several times, and he'd taken the cowardly step of asking his PA to give her excuses. Eventually, he took her to a crowded wine bar and told her that he felt he wasn't ready to see anyone yet. It would take an even more determined woman to put a halt to all others' efforts. In just a few weeks' time, Oliver would be swept off his feet and officially off the market.

CHAPTER 20

Harry lived on the first floor of a traditional stone tenement just off Leith Walk. The stairwell smelt of floral disinfectant, courtesy of seventy-two-year-old Lily Brooks who lived in 1F1. Every Friday, Lily wound her now sparse white hair into a loose nape bun, secured it with a single Kirby-grip, rolled up her sleeves and half filled a metal mop bucket with steaming hot water cooled a degree or so with half a bottle of Zoflora Hyacinth. She sometimes hummed 'Shama Shama', channelling 1967 Jane Fonda, as she mopped the worn front steps, the stone floor of the entrance hall, moving the Samenskis' second-hand buggy and Harry's bike to mop behind and underneath them, and the half-flight of steps that started the climb to the next two floors. By the time she mopped herself backwards into her flat, she was on to the best of Doris Day. On rainy days, she liked a bit of low-register Julie London.

Harry had moved into her flat two years ago, three years after Lily's husband had died. Lily welcomed the worryingly thin young woman to the block by baking her a batch of cherry scones that rivalled anything served at the city's swankiest tea rooms. She also lit a special candle at church for her on Sunday. Harry had featured in Lily's prayers most nights since, especially those when she heard the closing of two taxi doors around midnight and the building's main door being quietly pulled to in the wee small hours. When she saw Harry's current boyfriend kissing another woman outside the Filmhouse one Tuesday afternoon, she recited the Hail Mary for almost an hour in penance for the words she had uttered in the back of the number 22 bus. And minutes after she first saw Judy mouthing the door numbers as she trundled a suitcase along the street, Lily was sifting flour and dropping glacé cherries into a mixing bowl.

Harry had been using her spare room as a makeshift dressing room in which a desk, the ironing board and a defunct exercise bike now served as additional storage solutions for clothes, shoeboxes (some empty, some with photographs of the wrong shoes on the front) and a hatbox full of costume jewellery. The mattress – for there was no bed – had been made up with bobbly blue sheets and a faded pink gingham duvet cover. There was no pillow. There was no space for Judy to put her clothes, and not quite enough floor space for her to set her suitcase down flat.

'Just move anything that's in your way. Make yourself at home,' said Harry.

She didn't offer any suggestions as to where Judy might move everything that was in the way. She didn't apologize for the fresh turd in the cat litter. She didn't turn the music down. She didn't put the kettle on or uncork anything. After hugging Judy and squealing her delight at finally having her in the flat, she disappeared into the lockless bathroom for a pre-gig shower, waxing and exfoliation session.

Judy put the kettle on and switched it off when she saw that the only thing that approximated milk in the fridge seemed to be made of rice. Rice milk? Rice? Milk? She didn't even understand the concept, let alone want it in her tea. A glass of water would have to do. She put her phone on to charge and sat on the mattress sipping the soft water as she watched a fat woodlouse go about its business of eating Harry's skirting boards. Maybe she should have negotiated an extended stay at the hotel.

Thelonious Monk finally stopped playing and the sound of his piano was replaced by the drone of Simon Cowell's voice drifting up from Lily's TV. Harry's cat padded into the room. 'Oh, hello, Frank, I've heard all about you! Psst-psst. Come on, come here ...' She extended her arm and rubbed her fingers together to encourage the thick-necked moggy to come closer. He hissed at her, sniffed her suitcase, spotted the woodlouse and ate it.

Harry walked into the spare room and plonked herself down on the mattress beside Judy.

'I know it's a bit of a mess in here but I can move some stuff into my room. I've been meaning to have a bit of a clear-out,' she said.

Judy gave a tight smile. 'No, it's fine. I don't want you moving stuff about for me. I should really be thinking about finding somewhere a bit more permanent.'

Harry had liked the idea of having a flatmate, but the real thing – even her fabulous friend – seemed like an awful lot of trouble. Even so, a regular income from a flatmate would certainly help her to cut down her working hours so she could focus more on her singing. It would be nice to have someone to look after Frank on the weekends she was in Liverpool, instead of relying on Lily all the time. And she really liked the idea of having Judy around the place.

'You could move in properly, like a flatmate.'

Judy hugged her. It wasn't a 'yes'; it was more of a thank-you-for-asking kind of hug that morphed into the kind of hug that precedes a big cry, which put Harry on edge a little bit as she had a gig to get to.

Once Harry had left, Judy shuggied the cat from the centre of the sofa to make a human-sized space. He wasn't happy at being moved and gave a threatening trill. She further chanced her luck by drawing up her legs and tucking her feet under him. She leafed through the notebook she had taken on the weekend retreat. She tried to remember how fired up she had felt during that weekend, although she couldn't remember exactly what she had felt fired up to do. Now some of the notes didn't even look familiar, let alone make sense. She remembered telling the group that she was excited that she didn't know what she would be doing in a year's time. Even as she had said it, it had rung a little hollow, and she had found herself wanting the claps and whoops to stop as soon as they had started.

Here she was, months later, not knowing what she would be doing in a week's time. She wished she'd taken up Harry's invitation to go along to the gig, but she knew that she'd still feel lost wherever she was. She spent the rest of the evening deleting numbers and email addresses from her phone, and after she'd decimated her contacts, she emailed Patrick to arrange a Skype session. When Harry came home, she found her friend asleep on the sofa, fully clothed.

Hello and welcome to Skype, Judy Grace Taylor.

Judy selected Patrick's name and the six-note connecting tone rang out on her laptop.

Patrick's face appeared on her screen, smiling and familiar.

'Can you see me, Judy? Can you hear me?'

'Hi, Patrick. Yes, I can see you. Can you see me?'

'Yes, I can. And I see you've changed your name!'

'Back to my unmarried name. A fresh start!'

Their Skype sessions had been few and far between, mainly because she enjoyed going to Patrick's house as much as she enjoyed the sessions. During the 'remote sessions' (as Patrick detailed them on his invoices), she would occasionally find herself believing, sometimes for a couple of minutes or so, that she wasn't talking to the real Patrick but to some sort of super-realistic animated chatbot, and she would find herself testing his listening skills with swift changes in subject and the odd non sequitur. It was only the subtle twitch of his mouth that would reboot her and let her know that – on an unconscious level even Freud had not charted – he also suspected she needed more support than he could offer.

'How are you?'

'I'm in Edinburgh!'

'No, I said *how* are you?'

'Yes, I know. I was just saying that I'm in Edinburgh. I've moved.'

'You've moved?'

'Yes. I've left. I've come here for a while. Well, I don't know how long for, really. This is just where I am right now. I'm in Harry's flat. Harry's the woman—'

'Yes, I know who Harry is.'

'Yes, of course you do. Well, that's where I am. I'm in her flat. With a very smelly cat.'

'Oh, dear!'

'Well, I like cats, usually, but this one tends to use the litter tray a lot and it's right next to the spare room where I am.'

Patrick grimaced. People would often talk about the weather, the traffic, parking tickets and bastard traffic wardens, minor spats at work, inconvenient gym opening hours, cat litter – anything to keep satelliting around the real nitty-gritty.

'So, obviously, I've left Oliver …'

'OK.'

'I feel like I'm a million miles away from everything down there. It's so different. I feel like I can almost forget about Dad being ill, and Oliver suffering, and everybody hating me.

Does that sound awful? I don't mean I want to run away from everything.'

She rubbed her face. 'I sort of do. I sort of want to run away. Does that sound awful?'

'It doesn't sound awful, no. It sounds understandable.'

'Only to you. Believe me, Patrick, nobody else is taking this well.'

'The people most directly affected will obviously see things differently, Judy, but the heat will pass.'

'Oh, hang on, let me get a pen.' She disappeared off the screen and Patrick sat motionless, his face perfectly neutral, like a lovely screensaver.

'I just wanted to write that down: "The heat will pass." I like that. I might use it as my little mantra when things get really heated!' She made a note and underlined it.

'Feelings will be running high right now. Have you spoken to anyone down here since you left?'

'Just Rob and Paul and Gina.'

'OK, so you have some support?'

'Not really. Well, yes, I suppose I do. Yes.'

Patrick nodded, and waited for her to elaborate. Instead, she ducked off to the right of the screen to adjust the volume on her speaker.

'And a plan? Do you have a plan?'

'What – like a written plan?'

'Well, an idea of what you might do next.'

'I just thought I'd stay here for a bit and try to figure things out. Just think about stuff. I know I've had ages to think but I couldn't really think clearly while I was still living with Oliver and working in the same job. It was impossible even to function some days, as you know.'

He nodded again, and gave her a few moments. Then he said, 'So your plan is to take some time out? To gather your thoughts? Yes?'

'Yes. I need to see how I am, I think. I'm on a bit of an artificial high right now. You know – I've just arrived in this place and it seems so full of life and possibilities, but I can't just live in Harry's spare room indefinitely. I have to sort myself out and decide whether I'm even going to stay in this city or go elsewhere. I've been thinking about doing some private tuition – that's as far as I've got. I suppose I just thought about that in the car on the way up here. So I might see students just to have a bit of income, although I'd have to see them in their own homes because I don't have a music room here. I barely have enough space to set my suitcase down, to be honest!' She looked around the room. Almost everything she could see belonged to Harry.

'Are you sleeping any better? Last session, you talked about not getting enough sleep. You said you were getting by on three hours a night most nights. Has that changed?'

She had forgotten about the sleep deprivation – sleeping so lightly that she could hear a footstep on carpet pile, Oliver's breath as he stood outside the spare-room door, his alarm clock being set, his (once their) bedsprings contracting, his (once their) sheets being pulled over his shoulders. She even imagined she could hear the scrape of stubble on his pillow as he settled into position.

She had slept in so far as her eyes had been closed. Her breathing and heart rate had ceased to differentiate between night and day, work and home.

'I'm sleeping just fine. I'd forgotten about all that lack of sleep. God. How strange. Yes, I'm sleeping really well. I rather like sleeping in strange new places – almost like being on holiday.'

'Great. That's great. I'm glad.'

'I feel terrible about my dad. I feel like I've left everyone else to deal with it all.'

The guilt of buoyancy.

'Would you like to talk about that?'

'I feel like I've just swanned off without a backward glance. Not that there's much I can do. I was just there for Mum, I suppose, and now I'm not.'

'You're not physically there for her, no, but could you be there in other ways?'

'I could ring her, but I feel like I'm going to get drawn into an argument because she's really pissed off at me.'

'Yes, that's a risk.'

'You think I should call her?'

His clients often asked him questions like that, as though what he thought could possibly be more important than their own judgement. 'I don't think there is any should or shouldn't.'

'I could write. I'm better in writing. That way, it's not an argument. It's just me saying sorry and I want to be there to help. She doesn't do Skype or email so I can't do that.'

'What do you want to say to her?'

'I want to say …'

Tears.

'Sorry – I just need to get a tissue.'

She scrambled off the mattress and raced to the bathroom for a few squares of scratchy toilet roll. 'Sorry.'

'That's OK.'

'I want to say that I'm here for everybody, but that I need to get myself sorted and that I wasn't OK – even though I looked OK, I wasn't – and that they need to give me a break. You know, Patrick, sometimes, I think they think I'll always be fine no matter what. And I'm not.'

'Of course.'

Silence. Space.

'I wish I could put the situation with Dad on pause until I feel more able to … I don't know. I'm not going back, I don't think. And he's not that bad. I had a perfectly lucid conversation with him on the phone just over a week ago. He has good days and not-so-good days.'

'OK. So is it worth us clarifying some key points here?'

Judy nodded.

'You want to get in touch with your mum to let her know you've not just gone off, and that you're thinking of her and your dad?'

'Yep.'

'And you want to let her know that you want to help, but that you need some time to get yourself right first?'

'Yep. And that they should give me a break.'

'And you want to ask her if she could just cut you some slack. Perhaps give you a couple of weeks, at least, to adjust to this big upheaval you've gone through?'

'Yeah. Can we run through those again and I'll write them down?'

Patrick, patiently and slowly, listed everything once more.

CHAPTER 21

Judy had lived all her life in academic years. For her, the mercury rising and waking up to sunshine signalled the end of the year. The new year began in September. It was now June, and she gave herself breathing space by telling herself that she didn't have to think about anything until the end of August. Except where to live. Fortunately, Harry had a plan. Or, at least, she said she did. What she really had was a rough idea of how much money she could make by tidying the spare room and a very naïve idea of what it would be like to share a flat with someone she'd formed an intense relationship with just a few months earlier.

'It's really kind of you, Harry.'

'Look, just think about it. I'll clear out that room and we can even put a lock on the door if you like and—'

'Jesus, there's no need for locks!'

'And if you pay me rent you won't feel obligated to me.'

Judy mentally switched money from her savings account into her current account.

'Not the going rate or anything. Just something so you wouldn't feel obligated.'

'Right.'

'Say four hundred pounds a month?'

'Yes.' She was saying yes out of embarrassment more than agreement, but the deal was struck. Four hundred pounds for a room with no lock, an aggressive cat who seemed to shit for spite, a stained carpet strewn with mounds of Harry's clothes, shoes and handbags, and gappy floorboards under which, she suspected, lived several families of woodlice. Great.

She knew, of course, that there would be no clearing out of the room. She knew that the cat would climb on her as she slept and that she would wake up most mornings with the smell of steaming cat shit in her nostrils. She knew that she would have to buy her own pillow, duvet cover and sheets. And towels. She knew that she'd have to chew through Harry's experimental ways with quinoa and that she'd pick up every restaurant and bar bill as yet another thank-you-for-having-me. She knew that she would have to live with the dustballs or clean them up herself. And she knew, without checking under the sink, that Harry didn't own anything that had been advertised on television as suitable for cleaning limescale off baths. However, she would soon find out that Lily's apple pies and scones more than made up for the quinoa.

Much to Judy's delight, Edinburgh turned out to be the kind of place where she could stand on a street corner and see dramatic Georgian architecture and the sea to her left and a castle to her right, where she could hear academics discussing their latest work as they walked through lush gardens, where she could get a cup of coffee at midnight, then pay a fiver to listen to world-class jazz musicians playing three feet away from her table till three a.m.

Harry had introduced Judy to the Jazz Bar and it became a retreat. A place that had the power to fade out the real world. A place she could go to alone to disappear into a set list. She felt safe there. It helped that Bill, the owner, had the peripheral vision of a parent on a crowded beach. He stood at the end of the bar and knew who was in, who was out and who was doing what in the tiny loos. Even from behind a drum kit, he knew what was going on. Sometimes people would wander in, seduced by the music floating up the steps on to the street. They'd take a while to acclimatize to the darkness, order a drink, scrutinize whoever was on stage, vow to dig out their guitar again and leave in the break. Others would turn up en masse, ready for a six-hour stay. They'd order jugs of cocktails for the three tables they'd pushed together and keep the chat to a respectful level when the angels ascended to the stage. Judy's ritual was to find a seat, sink a couple of large Jack Daniel's, and let the strange beauty of this intimate basement wash over her. It would be her main summer vice. Until the Fringe started. And the Book Festival opened. And the city's population doubled over the space of a weekend.

June was a month of anticipation. Festival programmes were launched at the start of the month, and pounced upon by shop workers and bankers, braced-up teenagers and middle-aged couples who'd made it through another year. Students flicked through hundreds of pages and mentally prepared for that phone call to Mummy or Mother or Mam in which they would postpone going home for the holidays so they could rub shoulders with – or at least spot – their favourite comedian in the Pleasance Courtyard. Bibliophiles marked with red Sharpies the date on their kitchen calendars when they would snake around Charlotte Square for their annual fix of Simon Armitage and Ian Rankin. And, come August, when residents would be unable to find a seat in their favourite haunts, Twitter would sing with the music of little birds telling other little birds what they had seen. But, for now, the soft rain of June kept the city cool.

'So, when are you coming up to see me?'

Judy heard Paul shuffle some scraps of paper at the other end of the line.

'I fly out in three weeks,' he said, looking at his plane tickets, 'so some time before that – next week or the week after.'

'Whenever.'

'It's nice to know you're so excited.'

'I'm just saying whenever is best for you. I can do either week.'

'The week after, then.'

'What's up with next week?'

'Right. Next week it is. I'll check the trains and stuff. Shall I book into a hotel or something?'

'Harry's flat is really small and I'd feel a bit funny about …'

'Yeah, no probs. A hotel. Any recommendations?'

'No, it's all good, really.'

'A couple of nights? You can show me the sights.'

'Yeah, that'd be great. Stay three nights. Make one night a Sunday and I'll take you to the Jazz Bar.'

'Get you!'

'Seriously, you'll love it.'

'Next Sunday for three nights, then. Are you OK with me telling Oli?'

'Yes. Of course. How is he?'

'Better. I've not seen much of him, to be honest. I've called a couple of nights but he's been out.'

'Working late, probably.'

'Yeah.'

'What?'

'Nothing. I'm just saying, yeah, he's probably working late.'

'Is he seeing someone?'

'I've no idea.' He started to laugh.

'You lying sod. Who is it?'

'I've no idea, Jude. I think he's putting himself out there. I heard Steph Lewis had been sniffing around him.'

'What's new?' She snorted.

'I think he may have succumbed.'

'Oh, right.'

'What's up?'

'Nothing. I'm just saying right. Good for him.'

'Christ, Jude, you left him! You're not seriously jealous, are you?'

'I am absolutely not jealous. Don't be ridiculous.'

'Well, what's up, then?'

'I don't know. It just feels strange, that's all.'

It feels strange to be replaced, even though that's what I thought I wanted. It feels strange that the sensation of longing for something different wasn't about geography or friends. It feels strange that there is a border between where I sleep and where I was born. It feels strange that nobody here knows that I had my appendix removed when I was twenty-one, or that I'm allergic to raspberries, or that I can't bear to travel in the back of a car, or that I can do a headstand for a really long time and can hula-hoop for more than fifty revolutions. It feels strange to be anonymous, adrift. It feels strange that, some days, the only time I speak is to order a cup of coffee. It feels strange that I am nobody's confidante and that nobody buys me something in the sales that they thought I would like. It feels strange that nobody – absolutely nobody – sends me stupid chain emails about how chocolate is superior to men in so many ways. It feels strange that I can now buy condoms as part of my regular grocery shop without selecting the least judgemental checkout operator. It feels strange that my mother's most hectoring voice rings in my head at least once a day: 'You've made your bed, Judy, and now you must lie in it.'

CHAPTER 22

DESPITE HER BEST EFFORTS, Isabella had only ever seen Oliver in action in the courtroom. He reminded her of a slightly heavier, more rounded Colin Firth. She'd lost two cases to him in the past year, and was about to win the next. It wasn't about the winning, it was the sparring she was most looking forward to. She liked the way he always seemed so sure of his client's case – almost as though they were heading to the only possible outcome. She'd tried to initiate a conversation with him after the last case, but he had seemed dismissive and cool. This had had the sure-fire effect of consolidating her interest in him.

Isabella had elbowed her way to the front of the less than orderly queue that was starting to form for Oliver's attentions. The news that he was as good as single again had blazed through the legal set. And his new, slightly more undone, look only added to his allure.

Isabella was disarmingly lovely to his assistant when she dropped off a file that she 'thought belonged to Mr Worthing', and she was equally lovely to his other colleagues when she bumped into them. She squeezed every last drop of information she could from them, researching him over coffees, glasses of wine and expense-account meals. The day before she aced him in court, she gritted her teeth through strips and strips of expert salon waxing and made small-talk with the sweetheart who did the best manicure and pedicure in town. She spent hours having her hair relaxed and extensions woven in. She had never wanted anything so much without knowing the satisfaction of eventually having it.

Not guilty. The gathering up of files. Shaking of hands. Words of consolation. Of course he'd come for a drink. Why not? Yes, tough trial. Well done. Yes, well done. Shall we make it dinner? Yes, let's. Another bottle? Yes, we deserve it. Would she like to come up for coffee? Cursory glance at watch for appearance's sake. Yes, sure.

There was no coffee. Taking 'Talk Show Host' by Radiohead as her cue, she pushed him backwards on to the sofa and made a mental note to tell his cleaning lady not to go so heavy on the furniture polish. The smell made her think of bored suburban wives.

'Watch me,' she said. And she slowly peeled off everything she was wearing apart from the most exquisite silk *dessous*. She leaned over, her nipple four centimetres from his mouth, guided his hand to a silk bow and tilted her hips away from him so that the bow untied in one smooth movement. Oliver, now slack-jawed but tense everywhere else, held a piece of silk so light that he wasn't actually sure if he was dreaming. Now naked, she unbuttoned his fly. He needlessly jumped into action and silently cursed his clumsiness as he fumbled his clothes off. His shoelace wouldn't undo, *fuck it*, so he pushed the shoe off with his other foot and it hit something that clattered to the floor. He resisted the urge to check the damage and focused instead on the softest lips he'd ever kissed. Those lips had been buffed with a dry toothbrush and balmed every night for weeks. She inhaled and then licked the trial sweat on the back of his neck. She'd worked him hard all day and now he was getting his reward.

CHAPTER 23

PAUL HADN'T SEEN OLIVER for a fortnight, but had received a couple of cryptic texts from him that seemed to suggest he was back on the dating scene. One very late-night text suggested he was doing quite well. They had arranged to meet at the Victoria station bar before Paul caught his train to Edinburgh.

'You don't mind my going, do you?' Paul asked. 'I thought I'd go before I head off to the sun!'

'No! Give her my best!' said Oliver. 'When do you leave for Brazil?'

They were each halfway down a large glass of house red.

'Next week. A whole summer of football. Can't wait.'

'A whole summer of kids – I don't envy you, mate!'

Paul smiled. Nothing anyone said could take the shine off this summer. 'Anyway, never mind Brazil – what am I hearing about a new woman?'

Oliver pondered his budding relationship with Isabella. 'Well, I don't know that she's my new woman, exactly. It's only been a few dates. Do we still call them dates? I'm not sure they've been dates, strictly speaking. More, well …' He paused to find the right words but realized he was rummaging around in an old lexicon. Oliver had always been the kind of man who was more likely to discuss legal loopholes with his friends rather than what happened in his pristine and often lonely bed. And once he'd met Judy, he'd found that his tolerance for listening to conquest conversations was so low as to be non-existent.

'Sounds interesting. Anyone I know?' asked Paul.

'No. It's a woman from work. Well, not from my office. She's a lawyer. Isabella. French. Well, born in France. Lived here since she was a girl. Very nice. Black hair …' Oliver went on to describe her as though he were talking to a police artist.

'Great.'

'It is. Yes. It is. Can I ask you something?'

Paul checked his watch in the hope that he'd have to make a dart for the train. He didn't want to be asked any favours or be given a mission to bring Judy back.

'What if Jude decides she wants to come back?'

On the scale of tricky questions, it was a mid-ranger. He could take this one.

'I can't see it, Ol. Can you?'

'No.'

Two bar seats became free and they sat down. Oliver noticed Paul was looking a little less lively than usual. He didn't know how to tackle that. Previously, he could have left it with Judy, who would have got to the bottom of things. He made an attempt. 'Have you heard anything from Jen?'

'She's still at her parents'. Her dad rang me a couple of weeks ago to ask if I could persuade her to go to rehab.'

'What did you say?'

'She won't listen to me. I told him I'd tried to persuade her in the past, but she wouldn't go.'

'You're best off out of it, you know.'

'Yeah, I know. I had a BMW following me for a couple of days last week.'

'The dealer?'

'I think so. God knows what's going on.'

'Nightmare.'

'Yeah. Anyway …'

Amy Winehouse appeared on the plasma screen, pre-tattoos and bloodstained ballet pumps. She looked juicy and wild. The camera followed her upstairs.

'Strange, having sex with someone else,' said Oliver, as he loosened his tie. The wine was kicking in and the police-artist had been dismissed. 'When the time comes, it's strange.'

'Is it?' asked Paul. He glanced at his watch again.

'Well, after so long. I mean there was nothing wrong with me and Jude, but you get into a bit of a rut, and we'd sort of …'

'I think it's the same for most couples,' said Paul, hoping Oliver wouldn't stretch to details that Judy might try to prise out of him this weekend.

'Have you ever had a woman do a striptease for you, Paul?'

It was the kind of sentence that almost necessitated a long, slow puff on a fat cigar.

'No. Well, I say no – not your *actual* striptease. Jen walked around naked most of the time but that was usually because she was too stoned to realize ...'

'Jesus. I've never seen anything like it. Very impressive. I felt like I was in a film.'

'God!' Paul was fascinated but hoped he would stop.

'Then she undressed me and ...' He took his lower lip between his finger and thumb and rolled it. 'No inhibitions. A pile of clothes on the floor before you know what's happening.'

'Gotta love the French!' said Paul, cringing and curious at the same time.

Oliver moved in closer. 'Have you heard of the gooch?'

'Graham?'

'No! The gooch! It's the area between ...'

As Paul blanched, Isabella strode into the bar with the assurance of a woman wearing the kind of lingerie that needed to do very little by way of work. Paul coughed to check his voice and looked her straight in the eye as she approached them. She modestly kissed her prize, shook Paul's hand and Oliver gave her his seat.

'Well, it's great to meet you, Paul,' she said, with a not-entirely-convincing smile.

'Yes, great. We were just talking about you, actually.'

There was some vaguely humorous small-talk but Paul soon got the sense that he had suddenly become surplus to requirements. By the time he stepped on to the Edinburgh train, the couple had left the bar and were heading for Isabella's place.

Paul rang Judy from the delayed train. He could tell that Harry was there in the background from the slightly stilted way Judy spoke, or maybe he was just noticeably more laid-back than she was after half a bottle of wine. 'Look, Jude, it's easy. Don't come to the station. Go to the restaurant and I'll see you there. We don't have to lose the table.' He had planned to tell her about meeting Isabella but convinced himself he should do it face to face. In truth, his nerve failed him. He worried that, if he mentioned her, he would somehow reveal those potently rendered images of Madame standing completely naked in a little pool of lingerie.

When Paul had first told Judy that he thought Oliver was probably dating again, she had definitely felt some relief. She didn't have to feel guilty every time she smiled or, God forbid, laughed. And surely their once-mutual friends wouldn't hate her quite as vehemently now. Although she didn't want him back, it was still a little disconcerting to think of Oliver with someone else, and Judy found it almost impossible to imagine him kissing another woman, having sex with her, talking afterwards. Patrick had discouraged her from trying to conjure up such images but there was a slightly masochistic part of her that couldn't resist. And the pinprick of pain took the sting out of the guilt, at least.

Over the past few months, it had come to her attention that single women seemed far more focused on body maintenance than she remembered ever having been. Even Harry, who was in a pretty comfortable relationship, was no slouch, having endured no end of painful sessions with waxers and clinical pedicurists. Her recent vivid description of having her facial hair threaded frankly sounded worse than going around with a full-on beard. And there seemed to be complex relationship games with ever-shifting rules that people were playing all the way to the altar. She wondered if she'd ever sleep with anyone again, and what she would have to do in order to prepare for it.

The waitress who nodded Paul into the dining room wondered why her own dates never looked like him. He was dressed in a charcoal T-shirt, black jeans, a black pea-coat and was unravelling himself from a red scarf when Judy spotted him as she sipped her Pellegrino.

'Hello, gorgeous!' He kissed the top of her head.

'I've never had a bikini wax.'

'Steady on, I've not even got the drinks in yet.' He laughed.

'If you're *out there*, Paul, that's the norm now: bikini waxes, pedicures, exfoliating.'

'A few weeks away from my steadying influence and you're talking pubic hair at the table again.'

She'd missed him. He was one of the few people who could make her laugh at herself. Her shoulders dropped a few centimetres and she felt a smile spread right across her face. 'Get the drinks in, Mr Roberts. It's your round.'

He glanced up and the waitress headed over immediately. He ordered a good bottle of red, some bruschetta and olives.

'So, pubic hair …' He grinned.

'What's Oli's new woman like?'

'Ah … *that* pubic hair!'

'Fuck off. What's she like?'

'She's a lawyer. She wears frightening shoes. She has very smooth skin that has definitely seen a shot or two of Botox.'

'Botox?'

'Botox. And she wears stockings. And I think she wanted me to know that she wore stockings.'

'What?'

'I just met her before I got on the train. I was having a drink with Oli and she turned up. Much crossing of legs and adjustment of small dress.'

'Really?'

'Really.'

'She sounds very glamorous.'

'She's very foxy but not a patch on my darling Jude, of course. What are we eating?'

'I'm not sure I've got much of an appetite after that.'

He scrutinized the menu. 'I'm ravenous! Listen to this, fresh linguine with—'

'What's her name?'

'Why don't you stop asking questions for a minute and choose some food?'

'What? You can't tell me her name?'

'I *can* tell you her name but you'll become morose.'

'Morose? Over her name?'

'Yes.'

'Don't be ridiculous. What's her name?'

'Isabella.'

'Ees-a-belllll-ah?'

'That's her name.'

'Why would that make me morose?'

'She's French. All women are threatened by French women. Including other French women. Fact.'

'Still subscribing to *Nuts*, are we?'

'I've never subscribed to *Nuts*. I'm merely stating the truth as I understand it. Now, the waitress is making her way back to us so I suggest you scan the menu very quickly so we can order some serious carbohydrates and get down to the dirty business of finding fault with Oliver's hot new woman.'

As it happened, there wasn't much more Paul could say about Isabella – he'd been a bit dazzled by her so they hadn't spoken at length. He had limited information from Oliver – she was French, mixed-race; her mother was from Somalia, her father from France. She had been educated in England at some posh, all-girls school, although that was probably not where she had learned how to bewitch a man with a highly accomplished perineal massage.

Don't mention the perineal massage.

'How did they meet?'

'Not sure, exactly. Oli said through work. Oh, he told me to give you his best.'

'Did he? Well, I wish him luck. He deserves it.' She took a large swig of wine. 'I hope she can, you know …'

'Make him happy?'

'Well, I hope she wants the same things as he does. Marriage, stability, blah-blah.'

'She doesn't seem the type to run away to Edinburgh.'

'It's temporary. Eat your food.'

'How's your flatmate?'

'She's OK. She's not around much. She's often out gigging. How's Jen?'

'I rang her about some mail that arrived at the weekend, but ended up speaking to her dad – she was still asleep at two in the afternoon. From what he told me, she seems to be going through a second adolescence. Now she's lost the baby, she's off out every night.'

'So is it finished?'

'I think it is. There's a lot to sort out – the flat's in joint names and I can't afford to buy her out.'

'You have sauce on your cheek.'

'Your sympathy is much appreciated.'

Judy rolled spaghetti around her fork and pointed the bundle at him. 'You know my thoughts.'

'I do. I also know that you're prone to disappearing, you recently lived in a hotel for a while, you're unemployed or certainly under-employed, and your bikini area is probably in some need of tending.'

'I didn't *live* in the hotel – I stayed there as a guest in the world's smallest room. And what do you mean by tending?'

'Tending. I just mean tending.' Paul forked a mound of risotto, popped it into his mouth and grinned. Judy felt more relaxed than she had in ages.

'Where's this B-and-B you're staying at?'

'Stockbridge. It's vegetarian, apparently.'

'Really? No bacon butties for breakfast?'

'Nope.'

'Did you know that when you booked it?'

'Nope. I just checked the confirmation email on the train and there it was: vegetarian.'

'All this way and no bacon.'

'I'm gutted.'

'Poor you.' She gave an exaggerated pout.

'Poor me.'

'I can make you one if you like.'

CHAPTER 24

HAVING RARELY SET FOOT in a church unless it was preceded by an ungodly alcohol-fuelled stag do, Rob, of course, insisted on a christening with all the pomp and ceremony normally associated with a child much closer in line to the throne. The day he planned included candles, the burning and swinging of incense – despite discouragement from the vicar – as many choirboys as could be fitted on three rickety benches, a ruinously expensive christening gown for his fat screamer of a son, both sets of new grandparents on their best behaviour, two sober and honoured-looking godparents, Min sporting just enough cleavage to show everyone she wasn't too mumsy but not enough to put the vicar off his stride, and Judy looking contrite and emphatically alone or, at least, without anyone who resembled a new partner. He mentally ticked off each item as it met with his satisfaction, and each tick served incrementally to curb his anxiety.

Judy approached the church like a reluctant bride, circling the block a couple of times, checking her brightest smile in the rear-view mirror. She'd spent considerable time rehearsing a less dazzling version for Oliver but was concerned that the associated head movement was coming across as a bit patronizing. *Poor Oliver.* She'd dressed down for him and up for Isabella: a navy shift, a tomato-red scarf, bare legs, low-heeled tan sandals, hair with a few centimetres of roots on show, short, squared-off nails, pale polish, no rings, no other jewellery. Nothing new but nothing of sentimental value. She couldn't bear to go to any event without a sweep of black eyeliner, but the effect was toned down with natural lips. Her bag, which was far too bulky for the occasion, contained a pair of Stella McCartney sunglasses (no case), her purse, lip gloss, keys, her phone (on silent), a tiny Moleskine notebook, a retractable pencil and a small framed drawing of Rob, Min and the baby that she'd sketched from a photo her mum had posted to her.

She didn't recognize anyone among the group of people outside the church and wondered if (hoped?) she'd got the date wrong. Fleetingly, the idea that everyone had changed so much that she wouldn't recognize them fired along a neural pathway but fizzled out. As it turned out, the tall slim guy was Oliver, minus fifteen pounds of grief, and the luminous woman at his side was, really was, Isabella Bost.

Dear God!

Rattled, she darted into the church.

'Mum!' Judy wrapped her arms around her mother's neck and breathed in Annick Goutal's Eau du Sud. She had smelt of lemons for as long as Judy's olfactory memory could stretch back, and had graduated from Ô du Lancôme only very recently.

'Oh, you're *here*! At *last!*' her mother scolded, taking in her daughter's outgrown hair colour, the slight finger dent where her wedding ring had once sat and the smudge of eyeliner on her cheek. 'Come *on*, sit down, it's about to start!'

Judy squeezed between her parents. She rubbed her dad's arm and he took her hand.

'How are you, sweetheart?' Before she had a chance to answer, her mother leaned forward and flashed them a threatening glare. 'Ssh! You can tell us later. The vicar's about to start.'

Most of the way through the unfathomable and endless service, Judy occupied herself by thinking of, and reluctantly dismissing, a number of excuses that might enable her to slip out of the church and make her getaway. At least one of the scenarios involved Jesus actually turning up. She knew that she would have to stay, of course. She tried to spot people she knew among the strangers in the pews as she lip-synched the hymns and squinted her eyes to almost closed as people prayed. She steeled herself for having to *smiiiile* in the photographs, eat three courses of ghastly food that had been prepared to suit the palates and chewing ability of everyone present, dance like she was having *GREAT FUN!!!!*, answer questions with only slight variations on the short script she'd rehearsed in the car, go home with her parents and sleep in the room that she'd last slept in about two decades ago.

'... and, finally, Min and I would like to thank our parents for providing us with wonderful memories of our own childhoods. We only hope that we can do the same for Charlie.'

Judy was finding it hard to keep down the pea and mint foam. If she swayed slightly to the left – and the prosecco was helping in that respect – she could see Isabella's swingy hair. She reassured herself that the feelings she had towards the back of Oliver's new girlfriend's head had arisen as a result of genuine concern for his having to put up with someone so bloody animated all the time. Nobody in their right mind moved their head about quite so much. All this swishing and swinging looked a bit desperate, to be honest. There was no need for it.

'Hey, it's Auntie *Juuuuude*!' Rob plonked the fat screamer into her lap. He continued to talk with an exaggerated babyish pout that Judy found not a little disturbing. 'Auntie Jude's come all the *waaaay* from Scotland to see you! Yes! Yes, she has! Hasn't she? Hasn't she, Auntie Jude?'

'Why are you talking like that, Rob?'

'Because, Auntie *Juuuuude*,' he continued to gurn his words out, 'this is how we talk to weekle-cheeky babies, isn't it, Charlie-chops?'

Charlie responded by vomiting over his auntie's chest.

Something about the quality – or perhaps it was the quantity – of the vomit meant that no amount of napkins dampened with prosecco or sparkling water would remove it.

As Judy sponged herself down in the toilets, Oliver wondered if he should just man up and try to bump into her on her way back to her table. Isabella was deep in conversation with Min and he wouldn't be missed. He circumnavigated the room awkwardly, edging between chairs, making his way across the restaurant like a man trying surreptitiously to bump into his ex while his new girlfriend was in the same room.

'Jude!'

'Oh, Oliver! How are you? I was going to come over to say hello but I was just trying to get this vomit off my dress and—'

'Oh dear. Have you overdone it on the prosecco?'

'No, it was the baby … the … Charlie who—'

'Yes, yes, I know. I was making a joke. I saw it happen. We all did.'

'Oh, good.'

'So, how are you? Still in Edinburgh?'

'That's where your lawyers are sending the letters to, yep.' She had no idea why she'd said that. It was a pathetic attempt to be funny.

'Right. Well, it was good to see you.' He was rattled. He turned to head back to his table. Judy stopped him by taking hold of his arm – his rather buff biceps, as it turned out.

'Sorry, Ol. It's just that I'm feeling a bit awkward. I didn't mean to say that.' Keeping her hand in place, she stroked his biceps with her thumb.

Isabella had been monitoring the vignette in her peripheral vision but only excused herself from Min's endless riffing on the trials of motherhood when she spotted physical contact. She drew herself up to six feet in her heels, adjusted her dress to reveal a few more millimetres of cleavage and catwalked over.

As Oliver spotted her approaching, his head started to throb. He had been rather enjoying Judy's hand on his arm and was a bit peeved that she had to pull it away so quickly. His only consolation was that she'd have felt his new biceps.

'Oli, I think it's time to go.' Isabella raised her eyebrow on the last word, making it look like a question despite sounding like a very clear and unequivocal instruction. She gave Judy a cursory glance. She certainly had a trace of a French accent, but Judy wondered if she wasn't actually laying it on a bit thick for her benefit. Oh-lee, indeed.

'I'm Judy, hello.'

'Oh, sorry,' said Oliver. 'Judy, this is Isabella and, Isabella, this is Judy.'

Isabella swished her hair back, tilted her head and displayed the bared-teeth smile of a woman who had found her man and was keeping him.

Judy was reeled back to her table by her mother's gaze. Once she was within earshot, her mum started the grilling. 'What on earth were you and Oliver talking about?' In more than three decades, Judy had gathered not one iota of evidence to undermine her mother's claim to have eyes in the back of her head.

'Let me sit down, Mum!'

'And what was his girlfriend doing marching over like that?'

'I bumped into him on the way back from the loo. I think she was feeling a bit threatened, so she made her way across to us.'

'Threatened by what?'

'Thanks, Mum. Can we change the subject?'

The subject wasn't changed for some time, but her mum, dad, aunties and uncles seemed happy to talk about it without any input from her, speculating when they fell short on facts. Judy distracted herself by watching an entire dance floor of self-conscious guests milling as Tom Jones was shamelessly followed by the Smiths. Morrissey could always be relied upon to clear the floor of all but the most serious partiers. She had an urge to join her old friends, to flail about to 'This Charming Man'. She knew they'd have danced with her, too, because they were decent people, but she stayed on the fringes, watching everyone else having fun. Gina made an unconvincing effort to encourage her to join them, but was clearly relieved when she refused. Judy promised she'd ring her the next day to meet up for coffee before she left.

CHAPTER 25

THE SCENT OF ROAST lamb wafted under Judy's bedroom door, tempting her from under the duvet and downstairs. By the time she emerged, the sprouts were stewing.

'I was about to send your father up for you!'

'Well, I'm up now, Mum. Good morning. Morning, Dad.'

She kissed her father's head, which was half buried behind the *Sunday Times*, and switched on the kettle to make herself a cup of tea.

'I hope you're not going to be making breakfast now,' said her mum. 'Rob and Min and the baby are due in half an hour. The lamb's nearly done.'

'No, Mum. I'm just making myself a cup of tea, then I'm going to get dressed and put some makeup on. I said I'd meet Gina after lunch, then pop over to see Patrick, and head straight off from there.'

'Gina rang. I've invited her for lunch.'

It was one of those rare occasions when all six chairs around the dining-room table were going to be used. Nobody had ever thought about rotating them for equal wear and tear, which meant that four were now somewhat saggy of seat and chipped where sandals and boots had brushed and kicked against their legs. Under the dust of the other two spring chickens, there was gleaming varnish and bouncy batting. The fat screamer's vomit and tantrums would, over time, take their toll on the more pristine specimens but, for now, the boy was content to wriggle and gurgle from lap to lap, sparing the chairs.

All the best china was out in his honour, and his parents did a grand job of keeping him away from it. Saucers were fished out from the back of the big corner cupboard and reconciled with their more worldly-wise partners. The crystal decanter was proud to hold wine whose label would not have been an embarrassment had it been revealed. Despite a fierce steam-ironing, the folds of the tablecloth revealed the depth of the drawer where it spent ordinary days. A large salad bowl, deprived of goodness, held neatly cut chunks of a supposedly French baguette destined to be scattered to the birds. Frank Sinatra crooned fifteen *Songs for Swingin' Lovers* at a volume high enough for Dad and low enough for Mum.

The doorbell rang. Min and Rob and their bundle bustled in from the rainy doorstep, sweating under their man-made fibres. They had walked the half-mile to clear Rob's head and tone Min's stubborn baby belly. Pram novices, they had yet to acquire the sixth sense of steering wheels around missing paving stones, substantial rocks, dog turds, chewing gum and puddles, giving Granddad the opportunity to show his skills with a bit of kitchen roll and the anti-bacterial spray. The smell of shit was barely noticeable by the time the sprouts were drained.

Although roast lamb would not have been Judy's first choice of breakfast, it slid down with fair ease, chased by leathery roast potatoes, watery carrots and sprouts that liquefied on the tongue. She turned her wine glass upside down and caught her mother's eye as she did so.

'No wine, Judy?' her mother asked.

'Oooh, a little hung-over are we?' laughed Rob.

'I'm driving. I'm going back to Edinburgh later.'

The illusion of happy families was shattered by the articulation of a fact they'd all been aware of.

Judy's mum pursed her lips and flicked away her husband's comforting hand. 'What's the rush?' she asked.

Judy reverted to her sixteen-year-old eye-rolling, jaw-clenching, adolescent self. 'There's no rush, Mum! I just want to get back, that's all. There's no point in—'

'For God's sake, Jude! You've only just got back!' said Rob.

'Christ, anybody would think I'd been at the other side of the world! It's just a four-hour drive!'

Her mother rose from her chair and threw her napkin into her terrible gravy. She spoke slowly in an attempt at drama and gravitas, but she actually sounded as if she was enunciating for her grandson. 'I will not have the Lord's name taken in vain by the both of you at my table on a Sunday.'

The Lord's name had been taken and bandied about for years at the table, but nobody thought it was the right time to be starting a fire with facts.

'Min, can I leave you to serve the trifle? I'm going for a lie-down.'

And off she swept. More Marge Simpson than Joan Crawford, to be honest.

After the trifle and mugs of tea (the cups and saucers forgotten), the selfish and ungrateful daughter loaded her luggage into the boot of her car. She offered Gina a lift home, even though it was out of her way. It would be a better drive if she didn't have another recriminatory send-off, and she had an hour or so to kill before a session with Patrick. As Gina buckled up and tried to find the local radio station, everybody else took their turn to hug Judy under a huge golf umbrella held by her father. He had taken to carrying it around of late, and didn't like it to be out of sight. On this occasion, it made him seem rather on the ball and protective of his family from the inclement elements.

Overused phrases were breathed into Judy's neck about driving safely and taking care while unsaid sentiments sat heavy and undigested with the sprouts.

She winced at the unintentional tyre skid as she pulled out of the drive, the wet road saying what she hadn't felt able to.

'Are you OK?' asked Gina.

It was a question that people asked only when things clearly were *not* OK.

'I'm fine,' she lied.

'I know you couldn't really speak at home about it but tell me about Edinburgh. What's happening? Are you going to stay there?'

Judy tried to ignore Gina's doubly outdated use of the word 'home' and attempted to edit her response to fit almost precisely into the gap between the now green traffic light and Gina's house. 'I know everyone thinks I'm a bitch, but I had to do it.'

'Not everyone thinks—'

'And it was the right thing for Oliver as well as for me. I'm not saying he'll thank me one day, but at least he won't have to listen to another of my award-winning faked orgasms.'

'Well, there is always that,' a snigger of solidarity, 'and he seemed fine last night. Paul said he seemed to be so much better than he was when ...' Gina faltered as she tried to let her friend off the hook.

Judy's anger had subsided, and she took over the conversation, creating a narrative around Edinburgh that she would edit and use many times over. They stayed parked outside Gina's house for more than an hour, during which time Judy never mentioned that occasionally she suspected she had completely fucked up her life or that she sometimes lay awake at night absolutely terrified about her future.

'Good to see you, Judy. Take a seat,' said Patrick. 'I love Skype, but it's no replacement for the real thing, is it?'

Judy joined in the small-talk as she removed her jacket and switched her phone to silent. She sank into a chair that knew her and looked out of the window in the hope of catching sight of Patrick's cat.

'How has your weekend been?'

'Difficult. Awful. Everyone was at the christening …'

Patrick's cat jumped on to the windowsill and cried for the glass to disappear.

'I felt so far away from them. I couldn't talk to anyone. I felt as though whatever I said about my life now would inflame things, make them hate me even more or …' She put the tips of her fingers on the window and the cat brushed against where they were, flattening his fur against it.

'And Rob is driving me mad. He's being a sanctimonious prick at the moment.'

Patrick laughed, and a couple of his textbooks bristled and tutted.

'Jesus, you'd think he'd created some kind of superhuman the way he talks about this baby. And it's not about the baby himself – it's all about what Rob's done. *He*'s made a superhuman. Like when he helped Dad build that shed. No, it wasn't just a shed – it was a *workshop* – a workshop with power and Wi-Fi and a bloody coffee maker. Honestly, Dad just wanted somewhere he could go to get out of the way of Mum for the odd hour. He doesn't even drink coffee. He uses the coffee pot to get his cuttings going. It's full of green shoots and hormone powder!'

Patrick tried not to smile.

'And Dad's up and down. One minute he's perfectly fine – or he seems it, at least – and the next, he's accusing someone of stealing something that didn't exist in the first place. He … Do you mind if we don't talk about Dad? I need to talk about everything else.'

'Sure. It's been some weekend for you, by the sound of it.'

'Everybody hates me, Patrick.'

'Is that true?'

'Yes.'

He paused for her to reflect on her answer, then said, 'How did you come to this conclusion, Judy? It seems such an extreme idea that everybody would hate you.'

'It's how I feel.'

'OK. It's how you *feel*. It's not a fact, but it really feels like that, huh?'

Sometimes Patrick really irritated her.

'Let's just say that Oliver is a very good lawyer and knows how to get people on his side. And I don't blame them, but I also think that more of them might have considered how I felt. How it is for me. Not now, because things are better now than they were before, but I've gone through a lot to get here. And I know it looks, to some people, as though I've just landed on my feet. You know?'

Patrick nodded.

'I didn't … I didn't land on my feet. It's hard, you know. I'm on my own – really, *really* on my own, and they've just …' She trailed off, and waited for Patrick to form a shape around her shifting and darting thoughts.

'So it sounds like people took sides and most took Oliver's side and …'

'Not everyone. Gina understands, I think. And Paul – he understands, too. It's mainly the couples. Even my own brother! I'm not saying that everyone should have been on my side. I just would have liked some fairness.'

Silence.

'But people are not like that, I guess.'

Silence.

'I know that people just react and then find themselves in a position they can't get out of, but they were supposed to be my friends!' She pressed the tips of her index fingers into the inner corners of her eyes, blocking the tear ducts. 'For example, I could see some wanted to talk to me at the christening but they'd have thought it would hurt Oliver, so they didn't. I kept getting surreptitious little waves from them.'

'It can be really difficult,' said Patrick, 'when couples split and people's loyalties are divided. It sounds like that's what happened for you, too.'

Judy stared out of the window at the cat eating grass. 'Why do they do that?' she mused.

'I guess it's just a very difficult—'

'No – sorry – cats. Why do cats eat grass?'

'I think it's to make them vomit something they can't digest, like fur.'

They sat in silence for a few moments, watching the cat.

'What's your plan? What will you do about your friends?'

She raked back her hair and twisted it into a knot at the back.

All of Patrick's clients seemed to have been blessed with thick hair, as though they had his share.

'Do you think I should try to sort things out with them?'

'I don't have an opinion on that, Judy. What do you think? What do you want to do?'

'I don't know what I think, Patrick. Can you help me here? Can I just have some help? Please?' She dissolved into sobs. 'I feel so alone. Can you just …?'

'Judy, you need to decide for yourself …'

'Right!' She raised her palms and pushed them out at him. 'OK. What I actually want to do is knock on their doors, while I'm down here, and tell them what shit friends they've been to me lately. I want to tell them I don't really need their friendship.'

Silence. A minute passed.

'It wouldn't do any good. They were friends of *ours* – of me *and* Oliver – and there is no me and Oliver any more.'

She unfurled a recycled tissue from a rather dusty box.

'I think things will work out with Gina,' she said, 'and Paul, of course. But the rest of them …'

And so she ate a blade of grass for each couple, before moving on to the meadow that was Isabella.

CHAPTER 26

THE A702 IS A road that rewards those who frequent it regularly. It's not a road for novices, having a variety of speed limits, turns that bend like liquorice and more than its fair share of impatient lorry drivers. It starts with an arm-wrestling roundabout at Abingdon and ends with a polite smile from Morningside that soon turns into a great big snog from Edinburgh city centre. Judy wondered about the people who lived in the tiny villages along the road. Did they work there? If so, what did they do? Or were they commuters who found Edinburgh house prices too eye-watering? Wondering about the people of Biggar and Silverburn quietened her worries about her own life. Her first trip to Edinburgh had been a way of shrugging off her past, a leap and a toe-dip. This second trip, somehow, had more meaning. The heat of the separation from Oliver had subsided and she was thinking clearly and rationally now. Perhaps that was

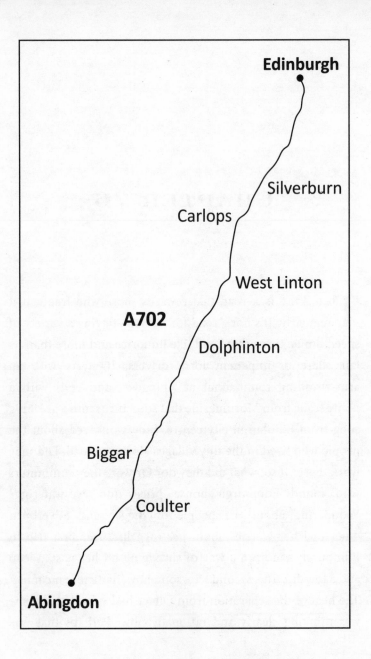

Edinburgh

Silverburn

Carlops

West Linton

A702

Dolphinton

Biggar

Coulter

Abingdon

what had upset her mother earlier today. She was no longer a runaway. She'd moved on.

When she arrived at the flat, the lights were off. Had it not been for the cat virtually holding its bowl aloft and doing a very good mime for Whiskas, she wouldn't have known that Harry had been out all day. On the cat's insistence, she fed it before putting the kettle on. The block seemed quiet yet it was only just after eleven p.m. She didn't miss the old Sunday night feeling at all – staying up late to eke out the weekend, ironing work clothes, remembering that she hadn't got around to cooking some sensible meals and freezing them. Sundays hadn't been all bad, of course – at least the car was clean, the sheets had been changed and the bathroom washbasin unblocked. The laundry pile had been reduced, the recycling had been pushed into already full supermarket skips and all the bills had been paid. Mondays would swing by with chat of the weekend; on Tuesdays there would be her session with Patrick or meeting up with Gina; Wednesday was quiz night at the pub; Thursday was almost the weekend and Friday brought the big shop at Sainsbury's, with indulgent treats for the weekend, or they'd gone to Waitrose if it was the end of the month.

She checked her emails from the warmth and comfort of her bed. Harry had sent one from somebody else's BlackBerry with URGENT in the subject line. She was in Glasgow at a gig and had lost her phone. Could Judy please feed Frank and email her back to let her know that she'd done it? There was an email from a potential new music student, asking to meet her on Monday afternoon. Another from Patrick, confirming their next scheduled session. Frank plonked himself on the mattress in an uncharacteristically charitable position that made it possible for both him and Judy to get a good night's sleep. Ten minutes later the lights were out and the block was silent.

No bread. No milk. No coffee. No wonder Harry always looked as if she could do with a good feed. Judy ran to the corner shop, cursing the rain and whoever thought that rice milk and chicory powder were foodstuffs. By the time she let herself back into the flat, her bra hooks were in danger of rusting. She peeled her clothes off, wrung them out over the bath, and took a hot shower. She couldn't wash her hair as Harry had seen fit to use the last of the shampoo and leave the empty bottle there. Was it a reminder for Judy to buy another or an attempt to cover her tracks by putting its disappearance down to evaporation? *Why am I analysing what happened to the sodding shampoo?* She turned the shower off and dried herself to the beat of its permanent drip.

Standing in the kitchen window, she could see forked lightning in the distance. She pushed two slices of bread into the toaster slots. A low rumble of thunder growled around the block. Frank stayed curled like a cottage loaf on the sofa, his ears occasionally flicking. Judy joined him, balancing her toast on a mug of tea, ingeniously saving herself washing-up. From her cosy vantage-point, the bay windows offered a panoramic view of similar buildings, many with steamed-up windows and lights on, and a glimpse of the Firth of Forth if she craned slightly to the left. She could see a daub of blue sky in Fife. In less than an hour, freshly bathed swallows would swoop back on to the streets, singing at a distinctly higher pitch than their country cousins, celebrating the start of a sunny afternoon.

Judy had arranged to meet a new potential student that afternoon at French Press café. On her way down the stairs, she heard a clang from Lily's flat. She knocked at the door. 'Lily? Are you OK?'

Lily opened the door, looking defeated and soaked with full cream milk. 'The carton just slipped out of my hand and then the bowl fell on the floor. I've milk and flour all over the place!'

'Let me come in and help you clear it up.'

Lily waved her in. A heavy mixing bowl sat on the kitchen floor, unbroken, surrounded by a flat cloud of flour. The half-litre carton of milk had clearly hit the floor with some force and the resulting splash was now dripping down the cupboard doors and one of the kitchen walls. 'It'll stink the flat out if I let it dry,' she said, surveying the mess. 'Look at it! How did it get up the walls?'

'Tell you what, Lily, why don't you sit down and let me sort it out? It'll only take a minute.'

Lily was tired. She nodded. 'Aye, right.'

'Where do you keep your cloths?'

'Bottom drawer.'

Judy opened it and paused to take in what she saw. It was neatly filled with quarter-folded tea towels, a pack of non-scratch scouring sponges, various kitchen brushes and dozens of cut-up and hemmed squares of old sheets. 'You're well stocked up there, Lily!'

'I like to stay on top of things and I've enough time to make sure I do nowadays.'

'I bet that wasn't always the case, though?'

Lily narrowed her eyes. 'I've always done my best.'

'No, I meant I bet you didn't always have as much time as you do now.'

'I've always had time for my kitchen.'

'I can see that,' said Judy, as she wiped the pitted floorboards.

'You'll need the disinfectant.' Lily pointed at the cupboard under the sink.

The opened cupboard reminded Judy of a sketch she'd once done for a school art project: 'A Domestic Still-life'. Brands that she had forgotten even existed stood shoulder to shoulder, lined up ready for duty: Stardrops, Sqezy, Acdo.

'Blimey, Lily, do they still make Acdo?'

'Oh, aye! I use it on my nets. I get it at the Co-op.'

Once the cleaning was finished to Lily's satisfaction, she insisted Judy stayed for a cup of tea and a slice of cake. 'Just as long as you don't have to be somewhere?'

Judy pulled out her phone to reschedule the next Chet Baker. 'I just need to send a quick message.'

The walnut and coffee cake looked terrible but the taste more than made up for it.

'I'm not so good on finishing, these days,' explained Lily, by way of apology. 'I used to spend hours icing and decorating, but my eyes and fingers are not what they were.'

Judy ate another slice. She felt it was the least she could do to reassure Lily.

Although Harry had been the one to suggest – almost insist – that Judy move in, there was a certain chill once the rent money had been spent. Things were bright enough during the week that Judy handed over a wodge of cash for the month – there was wine and much trilling around the flat – but she started to feel in Harry's way shortly afterwards. It was hard for her to put her finger on it, but she felt it most keenly when she opened the fridge to find all of her food had been consigned to the crisping drawer, or discovered that her damp washing had been taken from the machine and plopped into the sink on top of a couple of dirty teaspoons and the cat-food fork.

It occurred to Judy that Harry seemed to feel more comfortable with space in her relationships. She realized that the initial physical gap, in terms of mileage, had probably strengthened the bond between them (and perhaps that was also why Harry had chosen a boyfriend who lived hundreds of miles away), but now that they were living in the same space, Harry seemed to be trying to create another type of space between them: hushed phone calls punctuated with booming and somewhat forced laughter, perplexed looks when Judy opined about something she had read in the paper, and a million other things. Some days, it made her feel rootless and in free-fall. On others, she felt like a warrior, grazed but still holding her sword, making her way through thick forest.

She had placed postcards on noticeboards and in newsagents' windows all over the city, advertising herself as a qualified music tutor. At first, she saw students in their homes, which helped her get a good feel for the neighbourhoods and suburbs around the centre of the city. Bus numbers started to conjure up sea views, golf courses, boarded-up shop windows, graffiti or grand Georgian architecture. She knew the stops where she could jump off for a quick coffee, and the routes on which it was best to hide behind a book and make no eye contact. Lately she had started renting a music room by the hour in Stockbridge.

Without a regular job, it would have been easy for her to sleep late and mooch around the flat on days when she didn't have students, but she dreaded the dull torpor that permeated the flat around eleven a.m. and had taken up running before breakfast. This served two purposes: it meant she was out of the way when Harry emerged from her room (neither was a breakfast talker) and it gave Harry the opportunity to get ready in an empty bathroom, make breakfast in an empty kitchen and sit watching awful breakfast television without being judged. There was another reason that Judy ran. At first, it had been a clichéd attempt to make a fresh start on all counts, and she ran in a way that hurt her feet and jarred her knees. She bounced painfully along cobbles and cracked paving stones all the way to a lake, where swans seemed to smirk as she huffed and puffed around them. Sometimes, she would stop to get her breath and take a swig of plastic-tasting water. One morning, a man who looked as if he had been designed to run stopped to tighten his laces. He surveyed the beetroot-faced woman with her blotchy legs and leisure footwear. 'How long have you been running?'

Judy checked her watch. 'About twenty minutes.'

'No, sorry, I meant how many weeks or months?'

Judy, only slightly affronted that he had not mentioned 'years' as a possibility, exaggerated slightly. 'A few months.'

'It gets better, don't you think?'

He wasn't fooled, but he wanted to encourage her to continue. He remembered that he'd once felt like giving up every time he ventured out until, one morning, he realized that running had become the highlight of his day.

'Well, I'm not sure about that ...'

'Don't push yourself. Relax into it. Find your rhythm and it becomes like a meditation.' He smiled and gave a small wave as he set off with his tight laces. As Judy watched him go, she was awed by his grace, how lightly his feet made contact with the ground, how upright his stance was, how his fingers curled into a natural shape instead of a fist. Inspired, she set off a couple of minutes behind him, trying to relax her hands, find her rhythm and bounce rather than thud along. As soon as she stopped looking at the ground, the banana skins and dog turds disappeared. It would be a couple of months before she was running without thinking about the mechanics of it. After that, it would be plain sailing.

***

The most annoying thing about being a self-employed music tutor? Apart from the self-assessment tax returns, keeping hold of every bus ticket and receipt, putting up with pushy parents and their reluctant offspring, working on music of students' choosing from glossy songbooks or, worse, their own composition, the very worst thing was the no-show student. And the worst of the no-shows was the first lesson no-show: a full two hours. As Judy resigned herself to her six–eight p.m. being a no-show, she distracted herself from the waste of money in hiring the room, not to mention travelling to and from it, by scanning the accommodation section at the back of *The List* magazine. Two columns offered peeks into bright, south-facing flats, student-friendly bedsits and compact box rooms. She folded the magazine into her bag and decided to walk up through the New Town and back to the flat. On the way, she picked up some pasta, Camone tomatoes, bread and wine from Valvona and Crolla, along with a bottle of organic cow's milk. She hoped she'd be able to cook a meal for Harry and have a proper discussion about the arrangement. It was clearly time for her to move out.

Harry was already cooking when Judy arrived.

'Oh, I thought you were teaching!' said Harry, looking surprised as Judy appeared at the kitchen door.

'A no-show.'

'OK. There's enough for three! Would you like some? This is Jools, by the way.'

Jools gave Judy a perfunctory smile before quickly returning to the task of chopping onions. She was wearing sunglasses to protect her eyes from the juice.

'Hi, Jools. Yes, I'd love some, thanks. What is it?'

'Butternut squash risotto followed by one of Lily's apple pies.'

'Fantastic. I'm starving.'

Judy put her bag in the bedroom and kicked off her shoes. She could hear Harry and Jools chatting and laughing and felt a twinge of jealousy. She walked into the living room and pressed play on the CD player.

'Oh, Jools was going to plug her iPod in!' called Harry.

Jools ambled into the living room, sunglasses now discarded, and untangled a lead from around her iPod as its headphones dangled on the floor. 'Do you mind?' she asked.

'No,' said Judy, 'not at all. Go ahead.' She sat on the sofa and watched Jools from behind a copy of *Three Weeks*. She looked like the kind of woman who could wear charity-shop clothing without resorting to calling it vintage. Her purple dress was unarguably ugly, which made an interesting counterpoint to her beauty. Her face sported a million or so urgent little freckles, each a perfectly round dark brown dot. Her lips were stained red and the edges were blurred so it was hard to tell if she had a Cupid's bow or not. As she squatted to find the right socket for her lead, her dress hitched up to reveal a ladder in emerald tights. Her ginger hair was wound into an off-centre bun held in place by what looked like a Royal Mail red elastic band. Judy felt like a faded photo next to her, in her cream shirt dress that showed pale, bare legs.

There wasn't enough for three, as it turned out, although Harry made a valiant attempt to spread out the risotto to cover the bases of the mismatched bowls. All three women ate as slowly as supermodels, scooping up little mounds of rice and masticating for all they were worth. Once they'd finished, Judy gathered up the empty dishes and offered to bring in the apple pie. 'Is there cream or custard or anything to go with it?' she asked.

'Er, no, she just gave me the pie,' replied Harry.

Judy divided the pie equally: four o'clock, eight o'clock and midnight. She'd waitressed when she was a student, and tested her left inner forearm to see if she still had the ability to carry a line of desserts along it. She still had it. Carefully balancing the plates of pie, she slowly edged into the living room. 'Ta-daaaah!'

She froze on the last note as a hundred thoughts flew around her head.

Don't look shocked. Be cool. It's OK. You've seen women kissing before. Well, OK, you haven't seen women kissing before, but it's only kissing. Although, obviously, it's more than that. And it's cool. It's fine. You just walked in on something that is absolutely fine. Harry is gay. Don't be stupid! Harry has a boyfriend. He lives in Liverpool. He's a man. Harry's not gay. Jools is gay. That's why she's kissing Harry. Harry is not gay. She's just being kissed by a gay woman. It's cool. It's fine. People kiss. God, I don't want to get involved in this. What's going to happen next? I'm not gay. Definitely not. How can we all sit and eat this pie now? Fuck. I've dropped the pie! God, I've dropped *all* the pies! And Lily would have spent ages chopping apples and rolling out pastry and now the pie is all over the floor. Over my shoes and their shoes and the emerald tights. And now the cat's eating the pie. Who knew that cats ate pastry? And the lesbian woman – Jools – is on all fours. And we're all laughing. But I'm not sure we're all laughing at the same thing.

Occasionally, Judy thought she could actually feel the ground shifting beneath her feet.

'Christ, Judy, do you think I'm going to suddenly seduce you in the middle of the night or something?'

'Harry, please, would you just calm down? It's nothing to do with that!'

'Well, why are you moving out?'

'Because I need my own place. I want to live in this city properly, not bunk in with a friend like a teenager.'

'Judy, I don't think you know how much it costs to live in Edinburgh. The council tax alone …'

'Harry, don't patronize me. I've run a house before! I've paid council tax!'

'It's very different here, Jude. It's not like …'

'Yes?'

Harry rubbed her temples.

'It's not like what, Harry? You think I can't survive in this city on my own, don't you? You think I'm some little country mouse?'

'No!' said Harry, moving towards her, arms open. 'I don't think that. Honestly, I don't.'

'I'm making a life here, Harry. Don't think I'm going to scuttle back when I see how much it costs to empty the bins.'

'Look, it was a bit embarrassing the way you found out but—'

'There's no need to be embarrassed. I just think it's time for me to go.'

'But why, Jude?'

Harry wrapped herself around Judy and they held each other for a while as Frank peed loudly just outside his litter tray.

'I can't stand the cat, Harry.'

CHAPTER 27

ACCOMMODATION
New Town 1 bed garden flat. *South-facing bay window. No pets. Profs only. Refs required. £800 pcm. 07405 879 553.*

IN THE END, JOOLS proved to be a very good painter of walls and skirting boards – the kind of woman who didn't mind getting the odd bit of emulsion on her slightly odd clothes. Harry proved to be pretty hopeless at anything but making tea, compiling new-flat playlists and reading aloud the worst of the one-star Fringe reviews. The bay-windowed apartment was just off Dundas Street – a hop, skip and jump from Harry's place. The landlord had given Judy permission to paint over the red walls and green woodwork with any shade of white she liked. He'd refused to pay for repairs to the so-called working shutters, but was happy for her to do so. If she had any further questions, she was to contact the agent, who would be collecting the best part of a grand from her account on the first working day of every month.

'Are you going to look for a job, then, Judy?' asked Jools, stroking Chalk Blush 4 along a wall.

'Well, I'm trying to build up my music students, but I might look for something else part time now I've taken this place on.'

'Teaching?'

'Yes, probably. It's all I can do, really – except waitress a bit. Could try that.'

'It doesn't pay as well,' replied Jools, the voice of experience.

'Well, I'll probably do a bit of supply teaching and a bit of music tuition.'

'And Judy has her savings,' said Harry, as she put three hot cups of tea on the bare floorboards and leaned back against the edge of a not quite dry enough windowsill.

'I've been a *teacher* for fifteen years, not a Wall Street trader, Harry!' said Judy, as she scraped a stray bristle off the skirting board she was undercoating.

'I know – I'm just jealous! Tea up!'

Judy knew that she had to secure a more reliable income stream. Although she had a good year's living expenses in her savings account, her safety net was lowering closer to the hard concrete with every visit to the cashpoint. Oliver had relented on selling the house – there was now a for-sale board up, apparently. The estate agent had been supremely confident when she'd taken the photographs and measured every straight surface: she had enthused about the forthcoming relocation of the BBC to Salford and how all the media types were selling their tiny flats in London and buying substantial, nicely appointed, centrally heated and double-glazed properties like this one. They'd snap it up. No problemo. However, with each passing week, her tone had become increasingly mournful. The weather wasn't helping matters – too sunny, too rainy, too windy. The credit crunch was stopping people buying, of course. One week, she was sad to inform Oliver that the property market was dead. Most recently, she had blamed George Osborne for her inability to find a buyer or even a viewer.

CHAPTER 28

You think you know a place until, in the space of a weekend, its population doubles. Week zero is when many of Edinburgh's inhabitants leave for somewhere sunny and rent their homes to people who, essentially, pay the equivalent of six months' mortgage to stay there for a month. Household-name comedians turn up and perform their Fringe set to the locals for a fiver a pop. In return for a 75 per cent discount, the audiences forgive technical glitches, lines that bomb and a performance that ends precisely fifty-five minutes after it started. By the time the crowds arrive, the sets are polished and the locals can get the hell out of their gridlocked city centre for the next three weeks, leaving it to the tourists. There are, of course, those who dine out on the time they saw X perform in a small room to an audience of twelve, or listened to an impromptu jam session from a jazz legend in Henry's (when Henry's *was* Henry's) and those who quest throughout August to add such tales to their repertoire.

'Who are all these people?'

Judy was a virgin to it, and Harry – an old hand after four years – took great delight in her response. 'You've seen nothing yet. Wait till the weekend. Everybody arrives at the weekend. If you want a cup of coffee in the Edinburgh Larder over the next month, you need to get in there before ten a.m. or forget it.'

'Jesus, I'd heard it got busy, but my bus actually sailed past me today, full! People were standing!'

'Forget the bus. It'll be full of people who flash venue numbers at bus drivers and don't have the right change. And don't think a cab will get you anywhere. Get a bike or buy an umbrella and walk.'

'Seriously?'

'Seriously. And if you want to know what to see, ask around. Don't let some flyering drama student lure you into anything.'

Judy pulled out a ream of flyers, each vying to make the boldest claims about its show, its performers, its unmissability.

'Bin 'em!' Harry reached to take the flyers off Judy, to save her from herself.

Judy resisted. 'I'm not binning them. I'm going to look at them and see if there's anything I fancy.'

'You're Fringe fodder. You'll spend a fortune in cash and time you'll never get back, sitting in hot, smelly rooms seeing shows you can't believe exist. Mark my words.'

'Well, that's my prerogative as a Fringe virgin, so leave me to it.'

'Jools and I are going to something tonight. A woman dancing naked on stage while a man paints her. Paints her actual body, not a portrait. She dances around him and he daubs her with the brush. It's all based on *The Pillow Book*.'

'Sounds very experimental.' Judy's tone was mocking.

'There are still tickets if you want to come.'

Shakti had been a dancer since she was a child. It was her pleasure, her job, her life. As a result, people and life danced around her. Difficult artists would acquiesce with uncharacteristic ease at her suggestions, enthusiastic and able people would arrive looking for work moments after a linchpin called in sick, her stage lights never blew and, while she slept, a magical night-shift plumped up oranges with zing and juice for her breakfast, selected beautiful playlists for her favourite radio station, whispered in her kittens' ears the secrets of being cute, brought adoring audiences to her show and scheduled rain only for those times when she didn't want to sit outside. She had never suffered from a cold, a hangover, PMS or even a headache. She had danced barefoot on a stage around pools of water and splinters of glass – there was no time to clean the stage during the Fringe – not once making contact with any of it. She woke smiling each morning and delighted in her husband Jorg's body. She would stand in the shower, with her eyes wide open, twirling shampoo through her jet-black hair and washing her feet by raising them to chest level; when the gods were handing out neuroses and joint pain, Shakti was too busy dancing to collect any. When asked how she had been able to dance on stage with such joy and vigour shortly after her father died, she explained that she and her family had applauded him on his way to the next life, just as she would eventually be applauded to hers. Death held no fear for her: she might fall down a mountain tomorrow or live to a ripe and gap-toothed old age. *Que sera sera.*

In addition to being a dancer and the main attraction at the Garage, Shakti ran it every summer. She did so with a light touch, a smile here and a wink there. If anything went wrong, little angels would appear from the wings or the gods, happy to fix it. It was as if the universe couldn't bear Shakti to be upset or dismayed in any way.

Judy was spellbound during Shakti's show. From the moment she walked on stage and let her billowing red silk robe fall to the floor, most audience members had to remind themselves to close their mouths, to swallow, to breathe, to blink. It had been a long time since Judy had sat through anything an hour long without wondering what time it was, how long was left, and if she had any messages. Now, barely ten minutes after the show had finished, she was sitting in the easy company of dancers and artists, laughing at the little jokes that popped and fizzed around the table, and quietening when Sartre, Kant and Laing were dissected. Occasionally, the conversation would lapse into French but Shakti would unite everyone by translating the gist to those who looked lost. It was a million miles away from Banks Road, direct debits and defrosting the fridge. She'd accepted a glass of red wine from a belly dancer and a handful of canapés from a clown in full makeup. It was the Garage's press launch and everybody seemed to be invited. Reviewers came because they weren't pestered here by desperate performers or pushy PRs; performers hung around to be part of the scene and for respite from the relentlessness of it all. Harry and Jools sat intertwined on a plastic chair, kissing and nuzzling, occasionally throwing in their twopenn'orth to the conversation.

'An unemployed music teacher? Wow! How could we use Judy's musical talents, Jorg?'

Shakti liked to find work for the artists she encountered. Every Garage performer had to do a stint at the box office and help with the cleaning.

'Judy should play an instrument in one of the shows,' he said. 'She could do something with you for those six minutes the other show's under-running by.' Ever the technical director.

Shakti seized on it. 'Yes, Judy! You have six minutes to play something and I will dance to it. Perfect!'

'You're dancing in two shows?' asked Judy.

'Yes, one in the daytime – a traditional dance – and *Pillow Book* for night people.'

'Well, I don't think I'm what you're looking for. I don't really know anything about—'

'You will learn! You will pick it up! It will be interesting for you!'

'I really think I'd be overstretching myself and I wouldn't want you to be—'

'Judy, Judy, Judy! Those who do not move do not notice their chains. Someone once said that, and she was right. Now,

I'll leave it with you. We can work on it tomorrow. Bring some music or some ideas and I'll create a dance around it.' Shakti raised a glass to seal the deal. Judy felt as if she was in a film.

Harry and Jools walked as far as Queen Street with Judy, before parting ways to go home.

'Will you play?' asked Harry.

'No.'

'You should!' said Jools.

'I'd bomb.'

'No!' said Harry. 'And it doesn't matter anyway. You need to get into the spirit of things.'

Ah, the Spirit of the Fringe. How else could one sum up a city swarming with people who were prepared to stand on stage and get a killer review or be shot down in flames in the national press? People would mortgage themselves to the hilt, run up fearsome credit-card debts or donate a kidney to be a part of it. It was a month of the most outrageous possibilities that ran the gamut from launching stellar careers to pitiful disasters and falls from grace.

'No. It's just … I can't.'

'That's your chains talking,' said Jools, and, for a moment, Judy had felt her temper bubble to the surface. It was such a simplistic view.

Judy had never been interested in playing in public, and had little time for those students who whined on about nerves and stage fright. Now, she had the griping feeling in her stomach that she'd heard so much about. She thought about her old office. She pictured how it had been before she'd started to pack its contents into boxes. She conjured up her wall of bookshelves. Spine after spine of toppled block capitals, occasional publishers' logos and the odd face, slim, consecutively numbered journals, horizontal box files whose lids would open to reveal hundreds of thousands of dots on staves. It was hard not to feel a little lost without them. The shiny gloss of liberation was starting to weather.

The next day, Judy stayed in. There were cupboards to clear and Lily had promised to teach her how to cook a breakfast that would make any man devote himself to you for life. Judy suspected she was hyping up her skills, but was more than willing to play test kitchen.

'I thought you'd be out by now, watching them Ladyboys of Bangkok or something!' Lily sniggered at the idea of all those people showing off and parading around the streets.

'I want to learn about this breakfast, Lily. You promised you'd teach me,' Judy replied.

Lily smiled and opened the fridge. 'Let me see. Do we have all the ingredients?' She peeped into a couple of cupboards. 'Yes, all there. We're fine. I'll teach you once I've had my cup of tea.'

Both women pulled chairs away from the table and sat down.

'Why aren't you out?' asked Lily.

'I'm avoiding playing music on stage for a woman who would be dancing naked around me.'

'A ladyboy?'

'No, Lily, not a ladyboy! A woman. A dancer. She runs a venue. She dances all over the world. She's asked me to play on stage with her.'

'Shakti?'

'Yes! How do you know her?'

Lily shrugged. 'She comes every year. Always in the paper. You should do it.'

'She's naked on stage. I'm a teacher! I can't be seen to—'

'You're not a teacher any more, Judy. You're here now.'

Judy shoved the invitation into her anecdote stash, foreseeing several occasions when she could bring it out, casually. She realized, of course, that the anecdote would be improved somewhat if she decided to go ahead and actually take the gig.

I saw Judy when she first arrived. She'd been crying, you could see that, and she looked lost. She was silently mouthing door numbers as she walked along, peering at every door in the street. I was expecting her because Harry told me we'd have a visitor with a broken wing we'd be looking after for a while. I baked for her. I smiled at her from my window until she started to smile back. I upped the stakes with a little wave. Eventually, I got her to wave first. We spoke – not much at first – on the stairs. She sheepishly tiptoed over my mopped hallway as if I'd be less likely to run the mop back over half footprints than full ones. The time came when I could carry on singing with a full and open throat as she descended the eighteen stone steps between Harry's front door and mine. She once joined in but she didn't have much of a voice. I can't fathom who's paying her for music lessons.

She helped me clear up after I spilled some milk in the kitchen. Some would say I probably did it on purpose, subconsciously, to attract some company into my flat, but I reckon people who spend too much time wondering about what's going on inside other people's heads need to get a life of their own to worry about. The truth is, one minute I was baking and the next minute there was an almighty crash. You wouldn't believe the mess it made. She came in and helped me clean it up. Well, she cleaned it up on her own, really, while we had a wee chat. She was wearing the most awful clothes so I didn't feel too guilty about her getting down on her hands and knees. Girls these days don't seem to know how to flatter their figure. I've seen the most awful sights.

Anyway, she's not frightened of life; that's what I like best about her. She faces it. She told me she'd been numb for a long time in her marriage, but she's not one of those who go on about what a boring old sod their husband was. No. Although she's not got much time for this French woman. She gets a look in her eye when she talks about Isabella and her 'swishy hair'. Not that Judy's always the one doing the talking. No. She always asks me about my day, and when I can't find anything to tell her other than someone won a lot or the penny on Deal or No Deal, she doesn't go back to talking about herself. Sometimes she reminds me of how someone else won the same amount the week before. I can't keep track but she does; she's got it all upstairs. She listens and remembers. She's even had me talking about Joe and how we

211

met, how we danced, how I found him dead and cold next to me in bed one morning.

I didn't mean to tell her the bit about finding him dead, but she managed to open up a bit of me that I hadn't talked about before. And she flinched when I said it. Not like some people who would try not to show it and tell me to go on. No. She flinched in the way I do when I see those ads for children with no clean water. She took hold of my arm and cried into her other hand. I didn't cry. I don't cry about it any more. He'd gone and he's still gone and there's nothing you can do about it. There's nothing you can do.

But I look at couples now and I think: One day you'll have to face life without the other, and it changes you, it really does. We look the same afterwards. A bit lighter, perhaps, and paler, definitely paler, like we're becoming ghosts ourselves. You'd pass us in the street, sit next to us on the bus, and you'd never know that we'd screamed at a pitch we couldn't hear. That we'd lifted a grown man in our arms and shaken him. Shaking a man twice your size – you know about it once you get the sensation back in your body. You can feel how your arms had done something they'd never done before. And you find that you now have a boulder where your heart was that will take years to smooth down enough not to scratch against your raw chest wall. Judy's a long way off that yet. I told her so when she was crying but I'm not sure it helped.

There's no need for her to visit since she moved but she does. Sometimes she doesn't even call in on Harry, but she always looks up towards her flat as if she's trying to decide whether to go upstairs or not. A few weeks ago, she brought me a CD player

that she said she didn't use any more and some CDs to play on it.
I like it because I can choose what to listen to. I don't like anyone
else choosing for me. I didn't mind when it was Michael
Parkinson but he's gone off the radio now, hasn't he? Anyway, I
sing along as I'm baking and cleaning. (I like that this flat still
gets as dirty as it did when Joe was here. And I still like to bake
his favourites: cherry scones.) I find that, these days, I can hit all
the notes Julie London sings, but not the ones Doris Day reaches.
It's funny, that, because it used to be the other way around. I'd
struggle to get as low as Julie but I used to be able to match Doris
note for note.

Shakti bore Judy no grudge when she failed to appear for the
rest of the week. Eventually when she returned to the Garage to
see a show, Shakti greeted her like an old friend.

'Ah, musical Judy! You have one more week to come up
with something for me to dance to!' She smiled and Judy's face
burned in response. She couldn't. She knew she couldn't.

Judy had gone along to the show on the suggestion (a
barely disguised plea) of the Garage's press officer, Laura, who
was concerned about the audience numbers. Laura ushered her
in after introducing her to the performer's wife. As the lights
went down, Judy was aware that only two other people were in
the audience: the performer's wife and a scribbling reviewer,
whose silent mobile kept intermittently illuminating his face
with a blue glow.

The show started dead on time with the huge crash of a
cymbal. Slowly, inch by inch, a man wearing a bulky

chartreuse-coloured bandage loincloth emerged from stage left. He made his way to centre stage opening and closing his mouth in a silent roar. His hands slowly clawed the air and Judy could make out a tiny nick in his thumb. His body was covered in a chalk-like substance that reminded her of the stuff that had been painted on her chickenpox pustules when she was five years old. As the performer's crotch drew level with her face, she felt the urge to turn back to his wife and pull some sort of expression to convey that she wasn't getting any sexual kick from this particular part of the show, but it was too dark for that, so she sat still and silent as he started to unwind the loincloth as though it were a turban.

After quite some time, a slight figure clad entirely in black emerged from stage right and began to wrap herself in the coiled length of fabric, twirling it around herself slowly as it was released to her. Judy hadn't seen a man's penis so close up for some time. She noticed that it was slightly erect and started to wonder if it was strictly legal to be parading about on stage like that at two in the afternoon. She remembered that the forty-word entry in the Fringe brochure had stated that this was not a family show, but she felt it should probably be a bit clearer on exactly how far from family entertainment it was.

Another figure appeared. She was wearing a clear raincoat which served to highlight her naked body underneath. Thankfully, she was carrying a large white sheet, which she threw over herself and Mr Slightly Erect. All three performers stood still for three minutes in complete silence before leaving the stage. Judy checked her watch – only thirty minutes had passed.

The man returned to a pitch-black stage, somersaulting and rolling from one wing to the next. He looked like he'd had more chalk applied and was naked, save for a leopard-print posing pouch. When he stopped rolling, he crawled around on all fours, tracing a double white line around the stage with his forearms, knees and feet. Every time he passed her, she smelt sweat and the chalky paint, and could hear his increasingly laboured breathing. She felt it would be best for everyone if he stopped but he went on and on. When he finally came to a halt centre stage, there was another cymbal crash as he arranged himself into a cross-legged lotus position. A cool blue spotlight pooled around him. Millimetre by millimetre, he opened and closed his mouth and palms for the remaining ten minutes. The reviewer tripped as he sneaked out. His absence made the final applause somewhat sparse.

Judy found it hard to know what to say to the performer's wife as she left. The lights were up and the woman was smiling expectantly as she approached the exit. 'Lovely,' said Judy, as she sloped into the sunshine-lit lobby. She swiped up a discarded copy of *The List* on her way out and took herself across the road to the Filmhouse café for a particularly large gin and tonic.

It was filled with performers wrapped up in the micro-universes of their show, and tourists who slipped off their shoes under the tables. Judy hoisted herself on to one of the high seats, her back to the room, and had a private giggle about the past hour. She checked her phone. No messages. Nobody was looking for her. She was desperate to share the story, but who could she tell? She didn't want to ring Harry. Gina wouldn't get the whole Fringe thing. She drafted a text to Paul but eventually decided it wasn't really a textable story, so deleted it.

The next few days tumbled along. Judy's flat became littered with ticket stubs, programmes and flyers that she would have time to tidy in September. In the meantime, it was a rare hot, dry day in Edinburgh. The Meadows (the south side's Central Park) was teeming with sunbathers, ball players, kids on stabilized bikes and parents heavy with the tiredness of a full week's work behind them. Judy sat on a bench, reading and waiting for Harry and Jools, who were already half an hour late. As she waited, a text came through from Harry.

We have been seduced by a gondola of flyerers at the Pleasance! Going to a Fringe production of Rebecca set in Venice. 5 mins walk from where you are. Want to come? H+JX

She didn't. She rifled through the flyers she'd been given over the past half-hour. A jazz big band was playing at Summerhall – a cock's stride away – in a few minutes' time. She'd never been to an actual concert on her own before but, by the time the musicians had taken their seats and were tuning up, she had lost any shards of self-consciousness.

It was thrilling to hear real music again. Judy had become so accustomed to raising her hand every couple of bars to ask her students to 'try for that again' that hearing real musicians play a whole piece almost made her laugh with delight. She was transfixed by the flashes of gleaming brass held close to black suits and white shirts. The lighting guy, sleep-deprived from Fringe shows that started at zero-zero something and apparently nourished only on Shakespeare for breakfast, shone lights down the furrows of the black curtain. And the musicians, the beautiful musicians: on that day, not one was bald or paunchy or geeky (well, maybe a *little* geeky). Not one had cheated on his wife or treated a girl too carelessly. Not one sported an ill-considered tattoo that spelled the name of a former lover in dodgy Sanskrit on his biceps or ankle. Their fingers and mouths hypnotized every woman in the place. Faultless, they were. Like wee gods cramming the stage full of holiness and dirtiness, flickers of tiredness and jolts of genius. And the audience – moved to silence except when they applauded – were rapt, brimming with appreciation. They sank deeper into their seats with each tune, reaching for the hands of loved ones, feeling as if they had come home, heralded by a welcome the like of which they'd never heard before. And when the encore had passed and glasses were empty, they herded out into fresh air that hit Judy hard. She started to run, to separate herself from the sated.

The beat of her feet took her along streets and through squares. She dodged courting couples, exiting audiences and the odd *bon vivant*. Her breath was laboured and she felt pain in her ribs.

Some 346 miles away, as the crow flies, Jen's ribs cracked under the pressure of a paramedic's dedicated professionalism, and forced air whistled over her shrunken gums, past pitifully few teeth and increasingly blue lips, until she was as dead as her eyes had been for years.

Malty stepped aside to allow two solemn officers to come in and tell the parents what they already knew. And Mummy clung to Daddy as her womb contracted, and she wept for an altogether different gap-toothed girl. A girl with blonde pigtails and ribbons to match her gingham dress. A girl who didn't steal their money or Granny's trinkets, and didn't fall asleep drooling in Grandpa's old armchair. A girl whose arms had once been sunkissed and unpunctured.

When it was lowered into the ground, Jennifer Jarrett's coffin weighed barely more than the wood and the gold fittings.

CHAPTER 29

TIMING IS EVERYTHING. ASK any musician. Let's examine the work conference, the crowded bar on a Friday night, or the bus on a Monday morning. Let's say we happen to spend a heightened ten minutes with a person we feel sure could be the love of our life at the aforementioned work conference, in a bar or on the bus. And let's say we're already married or coupled up or have promised to procreate with the person we woke up alongside that morning. It's human nature that we immediately consign the potential love of our life to suspended animation, forever alluring and ready, wearing beautiful matching lingerie/cool boxers, smelling of unfamiliarity and promise. What timing! we silently wail, as we arrive home to the warmth and smell of the nest. And we sigh and sulk for a bit and tell our loved ones that we've just had a busy week or think we can feel a cold coming on. And, from then on, our loved ones are destined to be compared unfavourably to that cryogenic being every time we view them at their worst: drunk, premenstrual, sacked, cutting toenails, picking spots or examining whatever they've just pulled out of an orifice. Timing is everything.

Fabiana, for all her rollercoaster curves and gleaming teeth (not a filling in sight, not even a white one), had terrible timing. Paul could have done with her when he was nineteen and up for being swept off his feet, or when he was in his twenties and needed the kudos. It depressed him that he was past women who had recently been girls, that their coltish legs and dazzling looks weren't enough for him any more.

He would have loved to take her back to the damp north-west of England in the same way that he'd have loved one of his paintings to hang in the Tate or to score a goal for Man U. He could imagine the swelling of pride in his chest, the envy in other men's eyes, but he worried that it would fade with time, that he'd soon tire of slipping on spilled body lotion and eating stuff from plastic cartons, fresh from the microwave, for Sunday lunch. He promised her nothing, and her English didn't stretch to using the auxiliary verbs required to construct a sentence in the future tense.

Measuring intelligence is a fraught process. We can hardly agree on a definition, let alone how to quantify it. What is clear is that some people are underestimated while others are at the other end of the scale. Paul woefully underestimated Fabiana, as most people did. From what he could see, her beautiful mouth produced a meltingly sexy sing-song accent, but rarely anything funny or smart. She could fill a T-shirt so that the ribbing widened and narrowed in all the right places but she couldn't tell you where cotton came from. It was clear she was no wit, no wangler of words, but inside that fabulous chest of hers beat a heart that could have silenced Keats, Byron and Shelley. She could out-love them all. She knew when the people she loved were unhappy, and she also knew how to make things better. People felt good around her. She had a PhD in warmth and humanity.

Paul spent his days kicking footballs and throwing headers to eleven- and twelve-year-olds from all over the world. He had learned to say some key coaching phrases in seven languages, although he often encouraged the French kids in Italian and the Germans in Portuguese. Somehow it made no difference – he was understood. His evenings were less cosmopolitan. Fabiana, who had spent all day teaching girls how to hone their volleyball skills, had no desire to sit in restaurants a table's depth away from the object of her desire so they would eat in the comfort of her bed, surrounded by her mother's cooking and barely washed fruit. On the rare occasions Paul ventured off the bed, he would photograph and draw Fabiana, perhaps so he could later prove that she had been his for a summer. She was a willing model, which ironically served the purpose of tempting him back to bed, away from his lenses and pencils.

The day before Paul was due to leave Brazil, a group of Fabiana's friends dropped in at the small apartment. They filled the place with life and noise. One of the men put his iPod inside an empty glass and the farewell-party soundtrack kicked off. Bottles of wine emerged from carrier bags and rucksacks. Ice cubes were emptied into the sink and bottles of white laid on top. Reds were opened for breathing. Occasionally there would be a break from Portuguese to English, then back again. As the English phone number flashed up, Paul wished some of his friends could be there in person, not least to see the array of golden limbs stretched around the place.

He pressed the phone to his left ear and silenced the party by putting his right palm over his other ear. Fabiana, he saw, was watching him edge backwards into the bathroom, head down, frowning. Once inside, he closed the door and slid down the wall to the floor, searching for a verbal response to the inevitable words Jen's dad was croaking out.

'Thank you for letting me know. I'm so sorry.'

Nobody says anything original when they're told that a long-term addict has finally succumbed.

He decided not to tell Fabiana until after everyone had left. An hour later, her best friend, Maria, perched herself next to him. 'So, you are sad to go home?'

'Yeah. Yeah. I am.'

'You come back?'

'Yeah. Definitely.'

'When?'

'I don't know. We'll have to wait and see.'

'Wait and see what?'

'Well, I have to go back to school.'

She looked puzzled.

'I teach. I teach art.'

'But you love to teach the football. Fabiana says it is your passion.'

'Yes.' He laughed. 'I do love to teach the football. It *is* my passion.' He was stunned that he could laugh and use a word like 'passion' less than an hour after he'd found out Jen had died.

'So?'

'Well, I have a job. I teach art.'

'But you can have new job. To teach football.'

'Well, it's not that simple. I can't just leave my job and—'

'Why not?'

'Well, I just—'

'You should do what makes you happy and what makes Fabiana happy.'

'And what makes Fabiana happy?'

'You.'

For someone whose first language was Portuguese and whose English wasn't as good as her German, French or Italian, Maria didn't half make sense.

CHAPTER 30

ISABELLA'S TOP-FLOOR FLAT SPANNED the entire footprint of a large Victorian mansion. In the south-east corner there was a turret in which she'd placed a chair that faced outwards. From it, you could see the urban sprawl of Manchester punctuated by landmark phallic buildings, the white Wheel, and planes arriving at and leaving the nearby airport. Oliver was very impressed with this metropolitan abode. He sometimes fooled himself that he was entwined, or at least closely associated, with its glamour and sophistication. He admired the flat's décor, the dark wood, the enormous, unfathomable canvases, the sofas made for lying on. He loved the way Isabella arranged fruit so that it was just an arm's stretch away from wherever one was sitting. Despite tripping over piles of books, he appreciated their seemingly shambolic presence. He had never before met anyone who would live in such a place but he felt safe in that alien environment. Nothing bad had happened there.

'How would you feel about us getting a place together?'

Isabella had a knack for phrasing her plans in a way that made Oliver feel as though his input would be considered. He hadn't noticed this yet because he was still quite taken with the shapes her mouth made as her slightly accented words tumbled out.

'I just think it would make sense as we spend every night together, either at your place or here.' She stroked his hair and kissed his ear.

He had absolutely no chance. 'Well, yes …'

'Oh, I knew you would be thinking the same thing! We are so alike, Oliver.' More kissing. Deal struck.

Her period was one day late.

A week later, they were in an architect's office discussing how they could extend Oliver and Judy's house (never mind the technicalities – he'd take the house off the market right away and square things with Judy) to almost double its existing size. That evening, Isabella declined wine and placed Oliver's hand on her belly.

CHAPTER 31

JUDY'S STUDENTS – THERE were now six – had no idea of her recent upheaval or her more stable long-term history. To them, she was merely the woman who would help them to the next musical grade, pass an exam or master the tricky passages they were struggling with. She sometimes turned up with paint on her hands and clothes. She was, some suspected, a bit of a flake.

Fifteen-year-old Alice Latchin was a prodigious musical talent. Judy became aware of it within the first couple of minutes of hearing her play. When she sat on her piano stool, she would roll up her (real and metaphorical) sleeves and set about the keys as though she had been away from them for far longer than a school day. As soon as she touched it, she seemed to meld into the instrument, giving it life, giving herself life. Without the piano, Alice hardly seemed to exist; it was as though she spent her life waiting to be back on the piano stool.

There wasn't much by way of chit-chat when the lessons ended, but sometimes her dad would arrive late to collect her, and Alice would open up a little. Judy learned that her parents had been divorced for three years, that she lived with her dad, Nick, who worked long hours, and that she was often left to fend for herself and had become quite a good cook. If she didn't make it in music, she was thinking of training as a chef.

Judy accepted Nick's whispered offer of a drink because she missed male company more than she wanted to admit. She went straight for a hug when they met at the bar because she missed putting her arms around someone whose ribs had a greater circumference than hers. And she invited him up for a drink because she was interested in more than the circumference of his ribs.

Nick said yes because he had figured out what Judy would look like naked the first time he had seen her. He'd been standing in a cashpoint queue early one Saturday morning with Alice, when she had walked past. She was wearing jeans and a washed-out bottle-green T-shirt. Her hair was still damp from the shower, and she smelt of expensive soap. As she said hello to her student, he took the opportunity to make out the shape of her breasts. He imagined their weight. She'd put out her hand to him as the person in front walked away from the ATM and he had fumbled the shake, breaking away to get his cash. It had taken him three attempts to remember his PIN. By the time he was done, she was walking away. It was all he could do not to race after her.

She'd been relieved that the sex wasn't disastrous but disappointed that it hadn't been transportingly wonderful. He was slightly clumsier than she'd expected and she'd wondered if he was working through some mnemonic device to get her to the magical letter O. He was, she thought, rather like a student who had learned how to play their instrument but had not yet mastered it. At one point, he had forgotten her name and called her 'darling', which had made her snort. It had taken him a few moments to recover from that. On the whole, it hadn't been a bad effort. A good start, she thought.

She woke up with the smell of him on her sheets. He'd crept out in the small hours, citing an early morning meeting. She hadn't minded his leaving because she was tired and had forgotten how to sleep next to an almost stranger. There were limbs to negotiate (did intertwined seem too needy?), snores and wind to be kept in.

With no early appointments in her diary or expectant colleagues, she starfished and snoozed till mid-morning. When she emerged from the bedroom, she chomped yogurt and muesli over shuffled iTunes and considered her position. She'd slept with the parent of a student. Alice would, of course, be grossed out by any discovery of sexual contact between her father and her music tutor. Nick might or might not want to see her again, although he'd seemed pretty keen to see as much of her as possible last night. There had been no loose promise of a phone call or text. No email addresses had been jotted down.

It dawned on Judy Taylor that she had just experienced her first ever one-night stand. This revelation set off a firing of several billion synapses, as she almost simultaneously considered and dismissed names she had first heard in the playground, blanched at in the pub and had rapped along to in the car. While a deep, dark part of her brain looked for abusive names that rhymed with or alliterated to Judy, a more conscious part Photoshopped her head (with better hair) on to a perfect stereotype of a nonchalant city girl with a bathroom cabinet full of flavoured condoms, tingling lubes and Clearblues.

The sofa was starting to feel like a waltzer car, pulling her in and pinning her back. All the things she knew about herself were becoming hazy. The sound of metal grinding against hastily constructed wooden frames filled her temporal lobes but not her ears. A black-haired man with a glinting earring grinned as he spun her faster and faster. Her stomach lurched at the memory of the things Nick had whispered to her as she'd arched and stretched on the bed more naked than she'd ever been. Eventually, the ride slowed and her living room came back into view. Marc Moulin's 'Silver' rescued her, stroking her hair, soothing her. She got up, walked over to the window and looked out at the city with a steady gaze.

There was no rhythm to her life in Edinburgh yet. Her students averaged at one a day, keeping the wolf from the door, but nine a.m. and five p.m. passed like two forty-five p.m., unremarked upon. There was the paper to be read and coffee to be lingered over, of course. She knew she was one of the rare few who had the privilege of spending wet Tuesdays in the

Botanical Gardens and wiping condensation from inside buses en route to Foot of Leith Walk and Hunter's Tryst.

The next week, Alice showed up as bright as ever. Judy found herself scrutinizing her student's demeanour, accent and smell for traces of Nick, and wished she was fifteen again so she could ask if he really liked her.

He *had* really liked her, actually, but not enough to do very much about it. He was busy and thought it would be unfair to embark on a relationship right now. Yes, it was a line that everybody was using, but it was no less true for all that.

Contents of Judy Worthing's wardrobe spring 2011

1 very tired black wool coat

1 navy coat (too long, salt-stained at hem)

Navy jacket (carried twice, but never actually worn)

Black jacket (missing button)

6 pairs of black trousers (pretty indistinguishable from each other)

1 pair of charcoal trousers (for a change)

1 pair navy trousers (too short if worn with heels)

4 pairs of bootcut jeans (as advised by virtually every magazine Judy read)

2 incredibly uninspiring black skirts

1 green skirt with embroidered pattern

1 ivory skirt (unworn)

2 crashingly dull white shirts

1 black-and-white polka dot dress (which made her look like an aunt who drank port)

1 ankle-length grey jersey dress (for days when she wished she could disappear)

1 ankle-length navy jersey dress (ditto)

2 floral patterned wrap dresses (that even Oxfam would have trouble shifting)

1 navy shift dress (torn at seam)

3 unremarkable black dresses of varying weight and length

Folded items:

3 sweaters, 8 jersey tops, 7 T-shirts, 4 wraps, 6 cardigans

11 pairs of shoes in original boxes (2 pairs worn once, 4 pairs worn twice)

2 pairs of boots in shoe trees (yes, shoe trees)

3 pairs sandals (1 pair unworn)

8 bras (5 black, 3 white – all tired)

16 pairs M&S briefs

2 pairs tummy control briefs (one of which was excruciating to wear)

4 plain camisoles (2 black, 2 ivory)

Pack of 3 pairs barely black tights

Pack of 2 pairs knee-high barely black socks

4 pairs black opaque tights

12 pairs black ankle socks

2 pairs towelling sports socks

2 nightshirts

1 pair pyjamas

1 sports bag containing yoga and gym clothes, trainers, £1 coin and locker key

28 assorted bags

Locked compartment containing jewellery box holding 52 separate pieces

Contents of Judy Taylor's wardrobe spring 2012

1 very warm black padded parka
2 bright woollen scarves
1 pair black wool gloves
1 pair red faux-leather gloves (unworn)
2 hats (1 of which was bought when drunk)
1 pair navy linen trousers (right length)
1 Breton-style top (wine-stained)
2 pairs black trousers (well-cut)
2 pairs black combat trousers
1 pair black leggings (unworn)
1 pair bootcut jeans (for less confident days)
2 pairs skinny jeans (for braver days)
2 pairs boyfriend jeans (worn to death)
2 pairs black sweatpants (for indoors only)
1 green skirt with embroidered pattern
1 beautifully fitted black shift dress
1 jaw-droppingly sexy black silk dress
1 navy shift dress
Folded items:
4 sweaters, 2 jersey tops, 7 T-shirts, 3 cardigans
3 pairs shoes
2 pairs boots (one heeled, one for Edinburgh's winters)
1 pair trainers
1 pair ruinously expensive running shoes
6 bras (2 black, 1 violet [stunning], 1 coral [good with tan], 1 silver, 1 white)
14 pairs briefs (assorted colours and styles)
12 pairs black ankle socks
6 pairs towelling sports socks
1 pair pyjamas
1 pair black opaque tights
1 pair green opaque tights
1 pair tartan tights (unworn)
5 assorted bags
Plastic carrier bag containing sundry items
Plastic carrier bag containing dress borrowed from Harry
1 vintage handbag containing 6 items of jewellery
Digital camera
Metal music stand (folded)
Sketch book (full)

CHAPTER 32

Paul returned to college on an unseasonably warm September day. In the art studios, oil paints splurted out of their tubes too fast, and watercolours dried as soon as they were stroked on to the paper. In the staffroom, sunburned lecturers competed with each other over rambling tales about holidays in destinations that were, miraculously, all off the beaten track and blissfully free of other tourists. And each seemed to have befriended a local artist or café owner, whose name was dropped at every opportunity. Every conversation seemed to necessitate at least one difficult pronunciation. Once a winner was established, the loser was sought. In his absence, there were winces all round about how Paul had foregone a holiday this year to help young footballers in some *favela* or other. 'We must ask him how it went when we see him …'

Paul didn't have much time to share holiday tales, although he was sorely tempted to make everyone's hair stand on end with one of his drawings of Fabiana at her most glorious best. Instead, he was mulling over a phone conversation he'd had with Jen's parents that weekend. His answerphone had been flashing for a fortnight by the time he arrived back from Brazil: a sombre message from Jen's dad. He'd returned the call immediately, even though it was getting on for ten p.m. and he'd suspected they might be in bed. It turned out that Jen's family had been putting their affairs in order following her death. They had decided to give her share of the flat to Paul.

'It's your home, Paul. Jen would have wanted you to have it. You've lost enough.'

He had cried, possibly from being overcome at such generosity of spirit, possibly from missing Fabiana, but most probably because Jen's death had hit him suddenly like a medicine ball in the gut.

He threw himself into term duties while, thousands of miles away, Fabiana spent her spare evenings learning how to cook *moqueca* and coconut rice pudding with her *mãe*.

CHAPTER 33

ONCE THE COMEDIANS AND actors had left town, the wind blew in, depositing drifts of leaves at the base of tenements and in grilled shop doorways. Sure, it was bright, but the air was starting to flick freshers around their little pink ears. Young boys were now unable to hold on to achingly cold monkey bars long enough to swing all the way across until mid-afternoon. Squirrels found themselves wishing they'd made maps, and eyed their more rotund friends with suspicion. There was talk of snow further north.

Judy took a job in a coffee shop close to the university. It was only three shifts a week and felt like a big enough departure from teaching to allow her to feel she wasn't creating the same life 250 miles north, but it still had the comfort of students and lecturers popping in throughout the day. Sometimes it seemed that her old staffroom had been pimped with better seating, a coffee machine, good-looking young people and real academics.

Her brief, torrid affair with chocolate brownies was over within a fortnight and even her once beloved chai lattes soon lost their allure. Her clothes and hair smelt of coffee, and although the milk, espresso and flavoured syrups washed out of her clothes, other stains set permanently on her apron . She incurred bruises and minor burns most days. Perversely, she rather liked the sizzling little scars on her fingers and arms.

During slow periods, she and her fellow baristas would invent unlikely back stories and outlandish dramas around the customers. It was more satisfying when applied to regular punters: they could create complex biographies over several weeks, although if you missed an instalment you could quickly lose the thread. Once Judy had married off an elderly professor to one of his students – and it turned out that her colleague Andy had outed him as a former Mr Gay UK only last week. Judy argued that he'd already outed two previous customers in this way and maintained that it didn't stop the title holder getting married. By the time they'd moved on to someone else, the real Professor King was back in his study in a Skype meeting about high-energy particle acceleration with fellow Hadron Collider scientists. You couldn't have made it up.

Judy's favourite time to be on duty was when the university's evening classes finished, and revved-up students full of French literature, twentieth-century art and conversational German would spill in. They would crowd around the counter and make feeble attempts at humour, trying to order lemon drizzle cake in German, appreciating the aesthetic of the coffee-bean logo on their froth, and so on. They'd push tables together and latecomers would perch two to a seat. Music students would store their instruments under the table or lean them against walls. Now and again, a handful would pop outside for a smoke, very occasionally bringing the sweet smell of burned cannabis back in with them. Mostly, though, their drug of choice was caffeine. Their conversation and laughter reached a crescendo about half an hour after they arrived, steadying for another half-hour and tailing off at around ten thirty p.m. By eleven, only the students determined to find a friend or lover remained. The baristas wiped tables and stacked chairs in decreasing spirals around them – communicating the universal passive-aggressive signal for 'go home'.

Hey Jude am coming to Aberdeen next Thurs for mtg.

You free to meet up in edinb 6pm-ish? Ol

The text pinged her awake at seven fifty-eight a.m. It was Oliver's firm belief that the world would be a better place if we all had a scalp full of Head & Shoulders by seven a.m., and were out of the door by eight, puffing little Sensodyne-scented hellos to each other on our way to work. Judy blinked at her phone trying to make out the words until the backlight decided she'd had long enough. She read the text again.

She decided to respond immediately to show that, despite living without a landline and broadband, and working in a coffee shop that wasn't even Starbucks, she had her act together enough to be thinking clearly at eight a.m.

> Sure. Text me on Thurs to let me know exact
> time. J

Oliver's meeting ran over by two hours on Thursday, and Judy could tell from his increasingly terse texts during that afternoon that he was getting pretty stressed. She half expected him to cancel but realized he wouldn't have arranged to meet unless he wanted to talk about something important. Maybe they had a buyer for the house. Great. She could do with the cash.

Even though he arrived late, you didn't have to see which carriage Oliver stepped out of to know he'd enjoyed the privilege of resting his head on a white square of logoed linen while being poured a glass of red wine by some poor bugger. He strolled along the platform like a man in a sun-drenched park. Judy watched him with a degree of frustration, and was reminded of the times she had felt he was walking too slowly. Her mother had said it was a sign of ageing, but Judy knew it was just who he was. She had been oblivious to it at first, content to walk at his pace when they were courting, and suspected he might have speeded up around her for a while, until his body followed what his mind had already established: that he didn't have to impress her any more.

He started to speak before he reached her: 'I'm sorry, Jude – I just couldn't get them to wrap it up. I said I had a train to catch but …' She recognised the tone: he'd had a couple of glasses of cabernet sauvignon or some such.

'It's fine!' She smiled.

Neither knew whether to hug or just to occupy the same square metre as each other. In the end, Oliver rubbed Judy's arm in an avuncular fashion. She noticed his smile was the kind that preceded a tricky conversation. The last time she had seen it had been just before he'd informed her that they would have to cancel a weekend away because he needed to work. Plenty of water had gushed under the bridge since those days.

'I thought we should probably just grab a coffee on the station as your train home is due in …' she checked her watch '… about fifty minutes.'

'Yes, of course. Although, if need be, I could get a later one, change at Lancaster.'

If he was willing to let the last direct train pull out of the station without him, it was serious: either someone was very ill or – of course! – pregnant and would like to squeeze into a wedding dress soonish, which would hinge on someone else's willingness to rush through a set of divorce papers.

'… or a cold drink?' Oliver looked at her expectantly. They were standing at the counter of the café and, apparently, he had been reading the highlights of the drinks menu to her.

'Yes, perfect. I'll have a gin and tonic.'

'Sorry, we're not licensed for alcohol. It's just coffee or soft drinks,' said the man behind the counter.

Was this how it would be in future? Was she destined to always make a complete arse of herself in front of Oliver? Was this divine revenge for breaking his heart?

'Skinny latte, please.'

'Would you like a muffin to go with that? We have chocolate, peach—'

'Just the coffee, please.'

Oliver carried the tray to a small table and Judy cleared it of its previous customers' detritus.

'OK, you have forty-five minutes – go!' she joked.

'Ha! Very good! How are you?'

'I'm fine. How are you?'

'Fine, too,' he said, hooking his forefinger around the knot of his tie to loosen it slightly.

'Forty-four minutes.'

'I have a favour to ask you.'

She decided to make it easier for him. 'Is it about agreeing terms and getting the divorce through more quickly?'

'Well …'

'I'm happy to do that, of course I am, Ol. I want to move past the sticking points as much as you do. I'm sure we can iron them out.'

'Well, I'm happy to wave everything through, apart from the division of the equity in the house. As I said, I paid those big chunks off the mortgage with my bonuses so I think that—'

He didn't sound like a man asking a favour. She blew into her coffee cup and held it tight so she didn't throw it at him. He would earn more this year than she would in the next five and he was squabbling over percentages.

She interrupted his faltering stream of reason: 'OK, Oliver. Get them to write it up and I'll sign it.'

He visibly relaxed. 'I'm really grateful, Jude. I'm in a bit of a position, and time is of the essence, as they say.'

'Oh?'

'Well, I have a bit of news ...' He trailed off.

It was very unusual to hear an expectant father describe such news as anything but 'good'. Was he pulling his punches to spare her? Or was he a little sheepish about his clearly excellent swimmers?

'Isabella is expecting.'

'A baby?' He'd deserved that.

'Yes, a baby. And I want her to move in.'

'You're not selling? I thought we were selling. You're going to live in *our* house? You're buying me out?'

'Well, it won't be *our* house any more. We're having it extended – hopefully, it will be almost unrecognizable by the time it's finished. And it's very handy for the train and just around the corner from my parents. All our friends are there. I've also put a lot of hours into that garden so . . .'

His life revolved – and always would revolve – around these points that he considered fixed. It would never occur to him to change jobs, commute or make new friends. Now he had replaced Judy, he had everything he needed. The wallpaper and paint would be replaced only on Isabella's insistence.

Oliver would spend many future summers eating apples and plums from his well-stocked, mature garden.

Judy imagined herself as a little Lego figure being plucked out of a toy house, discarded by a fickle toddler, and Isabella being firmly slotted in.

She let Oliver find his own way to the platform. As she put on her jacket and watched him walk away, she wondered if he was happy. He didn't look like a man who had settled for just enough. He was heading for a first-class carriage that would take him home to Isabella and his semi-detached house with its enviable wine cellar and planning permission to extend the back with plenty of garden space to spare.

Judy couldn't face heading straight home. She fished her phone out of her pocket. 'Hello, Lily. Can I come over for a cup of tea?'

'Of course you can, hen. Now?'

'I'll be there in about twenty minutes. I'm at Waverley station – I'll walk over.'

She tried to make sense of her situation now. Mid-thirties, as good as divorced, working part-time in a coffee shop, living in a rented flat. Dwindling savings but at least she had a share of the house's equity coming to her – probably about seventy thousand. Dwindling circle of friends but there was hope on that front. Overall, not the scenario she'd had in mind for herself when she'd left school almost twenty years ago.

Lily had brewed a large pot of tea and put some slightly stale Morning Coffee biscuits on a plate. Judy had been looking forward to something more substantial and home-made, and couldn't face nibbling biscuits. She summarized the last couple of hours for Lily, explaining how she'd been defeated by Oliver's superior negotiating skills.

'Why did you give in to him?'

'Oh, I just want it to be over, Lily. I want to walk away from it. And I'm leaving it with at least something, which is more than a lot of people can say.'

Suddenly, Judy thought of her beautiful old sofa. It was one of a kind, made to her specific brief by a craftsman and his team of three assistants. It had cost a fortune – Oliver had complained at the time but had taken every opportunity to tell its story to new visitors and party guests. She imagined Isabella sitting on that sofa and felt herself starting to cry.

'Aye, it's all just sinking in. You have a good cry.'

'It's not that. I know it sounds a bit daft but … I had a sofa. One of Paul's mates – Paul's a friend of ours – had his own studio down a little back street. His name was Tony, and we designed this lovely sofa together … and the fabric I wanted wasn't upholstery fabric but he got another friend to reproduce my version of the pattern in the right weight of material … and it took weeks and weeks … and I kept calling in to see how it was doing, and every week there'd be something else about it to love … and this man, Tony, poured so much care into making it, and even his team would gather around to talk about it when I came in … and now Isabella's going to be sitting on my sofa and their sodding kid is going to spill beans and God knows what all over it and …' She was rambling now.

'Well, you mustn't let him have the sofa, Judy! That's your sofa! You can't have that woman sitting on it! It's yours!'

Judy blew her nose and took a deep breath. 'She can have it. She's welcome to it all.'

The beautiful sofa was saved from the skip by Gina, who carried it home with three friends. She would enjoy it for many years to come.

Oliver wasted no time in getting the papers drawn up; he pulled in several favours to get the lawyers to turn everything around at warp speed. Judy signed and returned everything on the day she received it. A few weeks later, her bank balance increased by £71,234.09, and immediately reduced to £71,134.09 when she took Harry and Jools for afternoon tea at Prestonfield House on the outskirts of the city centre. Magnificent peacocks strutted in the golden grounds as the party of three relaxed in a sumptuous leather-lined room. A refined, black-suited man apologized for disturbing them as he placed another log on the fire. Before he left, he topped up each woman's glass with a bit more Billecart-Salmon champagne.

As he left, Harry proposed a toast: 'OK, let's raise our glasses to a seventy-grand divorce settlement and to Judy. May she always have someone nearby to top up her glass!'

'And to throw another log on the fire,' added Jools.

CHAPTER 34

'IT'S NOT PERMANENT,' BARBARA lied to herself, to Judy, to anyone else who might judge her to be lacking in devotion to her darling Ray. 'It's respite, for me *and* for Dad.' She spared her daughter the unbearable details of what this was respite *from*, like how he had lashed out at her a couple of times, once knocking her over, and how she had found him mowing the lawn at four a.m. completely naked. Nobody needed to know that stuff. That was between them. Private.

Judy and her mother walked up to the entrance of The Gables. They held on to each other as they passed the enormous tubs of lavender that had been strategically placed at either side of the doorway to calm tense visitors entering the building and any residents considering making a run for it. The scent's efficacy was somewhat reduced now it was winter but, serendipitously, the residents were less likely to do a runner if there was a chill in the air.

Barbara struggled with how to prepare her daughter for what she was about to see. In the end, she left it fairly vague: 'Don't expect too much from him, darling. He's not himself. You need to be strong, Judy.'

In the entrance hall, Bob Dylan seeped out of an iPod worn by one of the livelier old gals.

Ray stood at the drawing-room window, his eyes fixed on Judy's car.

'Dad?' Her stomach lurched when she saw how frail he'd become since she'd last seen him. His skin sat on his bones with barely an ounce of fat between them.

He turned and smiled at, yes, *definitely*, it was definitely his daughter, he was sure. Judith. Judith.

'That's a shit bit of parking you did there, Judith.'

She had only heard him swear once before: on the night he'd opened the door to an eighteen-year-old biker who had reeked of patchouli oil and was proposing to take the fifteen-year-old Judy to Blackpool to see the illuminations. On that occasion, Ray had expertly strung together a particularly colourful collection of what Barbara called 'language' to conjure up a rather vivid picture of what he would do with Blackpool Tower to Geoff the biker if he didn't shift off the doorstep pronto. Unfortunately, that budding relationship hadn't survived the threat, even though everyone knew it was technically impossible to carry out.

'Ray, for goodness' sake!' said Barbara. 'Come and sit down. She's come all the way from Edinburgh to see you!' She arranged three chairs around a low circular table and Judy ushered her dad towards one.

'All that way just to see you, Ray Taylor, so less of the swearing!'

Barbara slipped out of her heavy coat and placed it on the back of her chair.

'How are you, Dad?'

'I've been robbed, Judith,' he said, staring at her with an uncharacteristic intensity.

'Robbed?' Judy looked at her mother.

'You've not been robbed, Ray. He's not been robbed.'

'They've taken my wallet. Every last penny.'

Barbara took his hand. 'Rob and Min are coming in at the weekend,' she trilled, as though nothing was the matter, as though her husband wasn't shrinking, fading, disappearing before her eyes. 'They'll be bringing the baby. That'll be nice, won't it? He's *so* bonny, that child.'

'You're bringing Robert in? Where is he?'

'Rob and Min are bringing their baby in, love.'

Barbara took a deep breath and forced a smile. Judy tried her best not to look horrified. Ray didn't respond. He looked out of the window for a few moments.

'That's a shit bit of parking you did there, Judith.'

'I know, Dad. I'll do better next time, hey?'

No response.

They sat without speaking for a few moments. Barbara stroked her husband's hand gently, rhythmically, soothing him and herself. A radio played in the background; Ray smiled and started to murmur a soft and incongruously sexy version of Leonard Cohen's 'I'm Your Man', note and word perfect. Judy dug her fingernails into her palms, transfixed as her mother stroked her father's thigh with her spare hand.

'You are,' she whispered. 'You *are* my man.'

Judy excused herself and fled as calmly as she could to the bathroom, where she gagged over a washbasin, coughing and spluttering. She turned on the cold tap, scooped up the shockingly cold water and held her wet palms against her hot face, wishing she had never seen the last ten minutes. Real life was seeping into her world like flood water under a door. She locked herself into a cubicle and sat down for a good cry, processing what was happening. It would still be happening even if she had not left Oliver, but part of her felt it was punishment for throwing a bomb into everyone's lives. She had never been touched by anything like this before. It had been plain sailing for thirty-odd years.

How could I have got to this age and not known that people live with this, and worse, every day? Deep breaths, deep breaths!

As she returned to the scene, she could see that her parents were still holding hands. It was something they hadn't done much over the years, or, if they had, she hadn't noticed. Barbara was laughing at something Ray had said and he looked rather delighted that he'd tickled her. They were twenty-somethings again, in a bubble, not a care in the world.

'Oh, Judy, your dad's just been telling me about something that happened yesterday. A birthday cake was delivered for someone, and they got the details mixed up. Anyway, the man who ended up with it had lost his specs and didn't read that it said "happy birthday" on it, so he just tucked in thinking it was a present from his daughter! He'd eaten most of it by the time someone realized what had happened! Can you imagine that?'

Ray was looking elsewhere now, disengaged from the story, and not sure of the facts any more.

'That's a bit like what happened to next door a few years ago – do you remember, Dad?' asked Judy.

'Oh, yes. Maybe it was next door,' replied Ray. 'Is Oliver coming? Where is he?'

'No, love. Judy's come without him today.' Barbara shot her daughter a warning glance.

'He's always busy, that lad. Always working away. He's a keeper, Judith. He'll look after you, mark my words. You'll never go short, will she, Barb?'

'She'll never go short, love, no.'

'How've you been, anyway, Dad?'

'I've still got my leg, unfortunately.'

'His bad leg. He means his bad leg,' explained Barbara.

'Are they giving you anything for it?' She'd started to raise her voice, as though he was deaf.

'I get nothing for it at all.'

'He gets painkillers. You get painkillers!' Barbara was doing a sterling job of interpreting and mediating.

'I bloody well DO NOT get painkillers!'

Barbara rubbed his arm. 'All right, all right. Let's calm down, shall we?' She reached under the table and pulled out a bar of chocolate from her handbag. 'Look what I've brought you.'

He took it from her, unwrapped it with some effort, and hungrily devoured the entire bar, choking at first.

'Take it steady, love!'

'Dad, slow down!'

People were starting to look. One of the care assistants stopped talking to another resident to watch what Ray was doing. He darted under the table and pulled Barbara's bag on to his lap. She wrested it away from him.

'I don't want it anyway, you selfish bitch!'

Judy's jaw dropped. Barbara, who had seen and heard much worse, slowly put the bag back under the table. As she sat up, she gave a tight little smile and raised her palm in a stop motion to the care assistant to let her know things were under control. Judy could see that her eyes were watering.

'Has your mum told you this place is haunted?' He was back to his genial self now.

Judy, barely able to breathe, tried to laugh, in an attempt to lighten the mood.

'No, she hasn't. Is it?'

'Aye, it's haunted. It's haunted, isn't it, Barb, this place?'

Barbara gave the tight little smile again.

'Oh, yes, we've seen 'em, they come up to the windows sometimes. Floating about in long frocks. You've never seen anything like it. Lovely. Not frightening. No. They're right friendly lasses.'

She hoped the right friendly lasses might leave her dad alone for a bit longer.

The drive home was surreal in that Barbara insisted on maintaining the veneer of normality she'd worn like a carapace at The Gables. Judy had expected her to do a Margaret Thatcher and crumble as she climbed into the car. Not a bit of it. Barbara faced resolutely forwards and chatted about the weather, various relatives, Rob, Min, the baby. Judy wanted to stop the car, to pull the handbrake up, unfasten her seat belt, face her mother and talk, really talk, about her father. But she understood that the only way her mum could cope with the horror of what was happening to him was to look elsewhere for constants and hope.

'I'm always here for you, Mum. You know, to talk to.'

'No, you're not, darling. You're in Edinburgh. And I'm fine. Min's going back to work soon and I'll be looking after little Charlie a couple of days a week, so that'll keep me busy.'

'I don't mean I'm here physically. I'm here to talk to. You can talk to me on the phone.'

'Thank you. I know. I'll phone you.'

'Mum, you can even visit me. You'd like Edinburgh.'

They stopped at the traffic lights.

'I know what Edinburgh's like, darling. Do you think we had no life before you? Do you think we didn't visit Edinburgh and London and even Paris, yes, Paris, before you came along?'

'I didn't know. You didn't say …'

'Well, you sneaked off like a fox! What do you want me to do? Recommend the Botanical Gardens?'

'The lights.'

'What?'

'The lights. They've turned green.'

Barbara tried to pull away but stalled. The man in the car behind beeped and Judy reached across to beep him back.

'Arsehole!'

'Language! For goodness' sake, Judy.'

Judy, Paul and Gina gathered around the pub table, each with their own stories gathered over recent weeks. Gina was delighted to be able to report, thanks to the shockingly indiscreet waxer, Tanya, that Oliver's new woman had a serious facial-hair problem. Paul had fallen in love with a Brazilian goddess. Judy had lost a house and most of a parent.

'We all have a bit of a facial hair-problem, don't we?' said Judy, finding herself in the odd position of defending Isabella.

'Not like this,' said Gina. 'Apparently it'd be a full-on Brian Blessed if left untended.'

'Brazilian women take waxing to a whole new level,' chipped in Paul.

'Wait your turn,' said Gina. 'She also has chronic athlete's foot. Can't get rid of it. Tried everything.'

'That's a comfort, Gina. Thanks,' said Judy.

'You're welcome. And, in my opinion, she's not a very good dancer. She's all about Michael Bublé and Il Divo.'

'Brazilian women take waxing to a whole new level. Have I mentioned that?'

'Yes, you have, Paul,' said Gina. 'Thank you.' She turned back to Judy. 'She just stands there swaying and wrapping herself around Oliver. Not a smile or anything. Humourless.'

'Humourless and hirsute. Nice,' said Judy. 'Do Brazilian women wax, Paul? Any anecdotes on that front?'

'Fabiana is as smooth as—'

'Before you go on, I want to say I think all of that is very dodgy,' said Gina. 'It's a bit prepubescent, a complete denial of womanhood, and I'm not sure about men who find it attractive, to be honest.'

'Oh, hello, has your feminism just kicked in, sister, now you've finished destroying Isabella?' mocked Paul.

'I'm just saying a bare mons is a bit dodgy,' said Gina.

'Well, it's not. I've seen it up close, and dodgy is probably one of the last words you'd use to describe her or her bits. Ditto "mons". Now, if you'll let me continue—'

'She didn't destroy Isabella,' said Judy. 'She was just trying to make me feel better.'

'OK, let's move on from waxing,' said Paul. 'I've just had the best summer of my life. I've fallen in love with a woman who talks *liiiike theeeese* and is *verrrrry* sexy. How cool is that?'

'Well, darling,' said Judy, 'while I'm thrilled beyond description for you, really, I'm not sure I can face too much detail because, in addition to this wine tasting like industrial paint stripper, my dad's got dementia, my mum's in denial, my flat's damp and my landlord couldn't be less interested because he's in the South of France in his lovely villa. On top of that, I've slept with the father of one of my students. He seemed like a fairly decent human being over drinks and in bed but turned into a shitty pumpkin at the stroke of midnight.'

'I've slept with men like that,' said Gina, unnecessarily.

'He made me feel like shit.'

'Yeah, I know. It's awful.'

'I thought your mum was coming to terms with your dad's …' said Paul, stopping short of mentioning dementia.

'She is, I suppose. She's just in denial about where it's all leading. He's not coming out of that care home, but she's still talking like he's going to be back to normal soon.'

'Maybe he will, Jude,' said Gina.

'Yeah. And maybe my Prince Charming, oh, and yours, come to that, will carry me off on a white charger, and maybe Rob's not really sleeping with that girl in the shorts from the gallery, and maybe Isabella's beard will trip her up, and maybe everything will turn out for the best. You can lead from the front, Paul. We'll all follow you into the sunset.'

They sat in silence for a few moments, sipping. Gina's phone lit up with a message from George.

Hope u get to see Jude + Paul. Will be back at 6. I'll cook.

You're dessert. Xxx

Gina tried not to grin, pass her phone around or make any involuntary noises.

'I can't stay long,' said Paul. 'I have stuff I've arranged.'

He was well practised in being able to place an icy distance between himself and Judy; a master of self-preservation.

'You've only just got here!' said Gina, looking at Judy to back her up.

'Thank you for the three-minute warning, Paul. Noted,' said Judy. 'I'm not behaving myself this evening, am I? Who knows what I might say?'

'I don't know what you mean, Jude.' But he did. They both did.

CHAPTER 35

HER LIMBS FELT LOOSER in Edinburgh, even though the city was now in the grip of winter. And she felt lighter, as if she'd shrugged off some pantomime padded suit. Her nerves were closer to the surface, but she had learned to take the shocks and bumps in her stride. Her sense of urgency to do something had waned and she fell into the rhythm of the city, walking around to the percussion of scaffolding being erected and dismantled, and regular fireworks. She was surrounded by people who might take part in one or other of the festivals but were not in a rush to do it this year. Maybe next year. It seemed to be no big deal here to put on a show, sell tickets, bomb or storm, and go back to serving in a bar come September.

Harry went to try her luck in London, and sublet her flat to Jools. She would send almost daily texts and chatty, upbeat postcards every two or three weeks that made Judy suspect that she didn't have enough to do and that her return was probably imminent. The city seemed more hers without Harry in it. One of her most recent memorable experiences had been paying fifteen pounds to get into a nightclub she'd left ten minutes later. Harry would have put her off ever setting foot in the place, but then she would never have stood at the edge of a dance floor watching a nursery of students dressed in eighties gear dance to Madonna and Duran Duran, their lip gloss pulled into unforgivably ironic sneers.

And there were the men. She discovered a delicious treat: she could sleep with someone and never tell a soul it had happened. The next day, she would wake up alone, having insisted he leave because she had 'an early start', and just go about her day, without wondering if he might call or if she should get in touch with him. Occasionally, perhaps on the bus or at a café table, her stomach would flip or lurch at a particularly vivid memory, and she might even laugh out loud, remembering some of the dialogue. It wasn't a long-term plan to continue but, like any treat, it was nice to indulge every now and again. And the beauty of it was that if she wanted to sleep with a man, she invariably got to do so. This soon resulted in making her choosy, and she started to take her time picking her bedfellows.

Inevitably, invitations snaked north to her – birthday parties, weddings, Christmas dinner, Dad's funeral.

CHAPTER 36

THE SUMPTUOUSLY FILMED *Back to Black* video is nothing like a real funeral. Of course it isn't. First of all, a real funeral is in colour, which means you're faced with a lot of red noses and eyes. Also, no brand of eyeliner, however much you trowel on, is ever going to get you through a funeral if you really cared about the person in the coffin. People do walk around in slow motion, though, so they got that right.

The church was filled with people who had come to celebrate the life of Raymond Arthur Taylor, who had died of a heart attack on Valentine's Day. His family was in no fit state to stand, let alone celebrate anything. The heads of those in the front pews were bowed, and plain white handkerchiefs were very much in evidence. The heads of those in the middle rows were tilted slightly, and turned to each other more frequently than at the front. At the back, babies were bounced and jostled and bribed with sugary confections in the hope that they wouldn't kick off. Everyone over fourteen wore black – this was no time to break with tradition. Some of the younger members of the congregation had made bold decisions that morning about their future wardrobes based on their funeral look.

Barbara's knees weren't what they used to be, so Rob and Judy took an elbow apiece as she stepped out of the blackest of cars, and steered her along the never-ending aisle edged with pursed lips and muffled sobs. As she reached the front of the church, she fainted. A gasp rippled backwards and Dr Kahan hurriedly excused himself from his pew and made his way sharpish to his patient. He knelt and brought her round. Her first words were protests at an ambulance being called. She was fine, she was fine. Judy tried and tried not to vomit and even took to praying at one point. Rob stood behind the lectern and made eye contact with no one as he talked about what a fine man his dad had been. What a father. What a granddad. What a role model. What a teacher. What a husband. What a dancer. What a carver of Christmas turkeys.

Everybody cried except the babies.

The vicar knew everybody, if not by name then from the flower arrangers' gossip. He shook hands and held papery fingertips, nodded and agreed. It was all a terrible shame, yes. A lovely man, yes. Too young, yes, too young. At peace, at rest now, yes.

Some days passed.

There are those who are comforted by the idea of going through five stages of grief before emerging whole again, and those who know that it's possible to fight so hard against mourning that it doesn't take place. Some maintain relationships with the dead, talking to them in the physical and metaphorical darkness and listening for answers. And while we may look to others for indications of how to deal with the finality of death, grieving is a unique and personal process that may indeed comprise five stages, but is as likely to consist of one or hundreds. Some feel safer maintaining a stiff upper lip, others drink themselves into the solace of oblivion, and many more throw themselves into the mine-black darkness of heartbreaking pain and emptiness.

'I don't know what to do with his clothes.' Barbara the widow was shrinking. Even her voice was tiny as she spoke from a corner of the sofa they'd once had sex on after watching something on Channel 4 late one night. Her husband was gone and her waistline was coming back. The bloody irony.

'We'll sort it out, Mum. Rob's coming over later. Don't worry,' said Judy, who was exhausted from days of crying and trying not to.

'Will he have had some lunch? Can you make him something?'

'He'll probably have eaten, Mum, but I can do him a sandwich if he's hungry.'

'There's some roast beef, I think. Or he might want something hot. I don't know what's in.'

'It's fine, Mum. I'll sort him out.'

'I don't know whether to send it all to the charity shop or ...' Barbara crumbled again. She had no resilience, no ability to self-soothe. She would bawl like a baby when nobody was around, and was barely able to regulate herself even in company.

The house was still full of undetonated mines: notes in Ray's handwriting on the pad by the telephone, mail on the doormat every morning, his favourite jam, his memory foam pillow. Each explosion would tear her in half. He was all she had known. Although he'd been in The Gables for three months, Barbara hadn't yet edited him out of the house because, in a part of her brain that didn't accept questions, he would be home again one day. She couldn't mourn because she couldn't believe he had gone. For good. For ever. She would *never* see him again. It was over. She was alone.

In a few weeks' time, a friend would tell her about the five stages of grief and, with that as a map, it would dawn on her that she was in stage one – denial – and was ready for stage two – anger. She would be able to place a foot hesitantly on the path to feeling OK again. For Barbara, the idea that she was only four steps away from acceptance was a lifeline. Four steps. Just four steps. She could do that.

'We thought you might want to move back in for a while – you know, look after Mum,' said Rob.

The sibling instinct to launch herself bodily at her brother for his stupid and selfish suggestion manifested itself as a physical jerk.

'It's not like you have a proper job up there. You can work in a coffee shop here, or Min can find you something.'

'I want to keep this shirt. It's the one he wore to Charlie's christening, do you remember? That was the last time he seemed normal. We had a bit of a giggle together at Mum and Auntie Jo gossiping about some old relative or other. Funny. He was funny that day. He got better with age, didn't he? Once we were settled and he stopped worrying about who we might bring home.' Judy bunched up the shirt and buried her face in it, inhaling the months away.

'Yeah, have the shirt. I'm gonna take his favourite cufflinks and his watch. I think the rest should just go.'

'We should keep some things for Mum. His dancing shoes, maybe?'

'Yeah. Let's start filling some bags. Let's get this done.'

'I'm not coming back, Rob.'

They packed in silence for a few moments, carefully folding trousers hand-hemmed to fit short legs, rolling ties of various widths that chronicled the fashions of the decades he'd lived through. Shoes were paired by tying the laces together, then placed in carrier bags before being put into a large sack.

'I'll take these, too.' Judy braceleted two expandable metal sleeve bands on her wrist.

'Nobody's asking you to come back, Jude. I'm just saying we think you should come and stay for a bit.'

'Who is this "we" you're talking about?'

'Me and Min. We both think—'

'It's got fuck-all to do with Min! What's she sticking her oar in for? She knows nothing about my life, Rob, and neither do you, so you can get off my back and you can tell Min that she doesn't get a vote on this one. Who does she think she is? Who do you think you are? God, I'm sick to death of people trying to—'

'Is everything all right?' Barbara's voice somehow cut through the rant.

'Yes,' they shouted in unison, teenagers again.

'Shall I make a cup of tea?'

'Yes, please,' said Judy, knowing it would be a pleasure rather than a chore for her mother to lay out a tray of tea and biscuits.

They stood eyeball to eyeball until they heard Barbara move from the foot of the stairs.

Judy jabbed her forefinger millimetres away from Rob's face. 'I am not having this discussion again. I am *not* coming back,' she hissed.

'Very fucking sensitive of you, Jude, leaving Mum like this.'

She tried to hit him with a tied pair of Ray's brogues but he grabbed her wrist and the shoes dangled mid-air. 'You need to sort your life out,' said Rob, as he took the shoes from her and slowly wrapped them in a carrier bag.

'Yeah. I need to get married, have a kid and start sleeping with someone else. Is that the kind of sorted you're talking about?'

'What?'

'The tart with the shorts – I know all about her, Rob.'

Rob grabbed her shoulders and their noses touched. His breath smelt like home.

'You. Know. Fuck. All.'

Judy and Patrick had come to an arrangement that suited them both. They would speak once a month either by Skype or, if she was in the area, as she was now, face to face, even if it was on a Sunday. She was the only client he spoke to at weekends.

'So I'm probably wrong about the woman in the shorts. I don't know. What do you think?'

'What do I think about the woman in the shorts?' asked Patrick.

'Do you think it's none of my business?'

'I'm wondering why we're talking about the woman in the shorts so soon after your dad's passed away.'

'Why do people say that? "Passed away"?'

'So soon after your dad's died. Sorry.'

'Because it's easier to talk about the woman in shorts and I really don't want to talk about my dad. I'm all talked out about him. I'm sick of crying. I'm absolutely empty and I wanted to come here and leave feeling a bit better.'

'I don't have a magic wand, Judy.'

They sat in silence for a few moments.

'I wish I had a magic wand. I wish I could make Mum better. I wish . . .'

Patrick's cat was sitting on the outside windowsill, its fur flattened against the window. Judy could see lines of its white flesh where the fur had parted. 'Can the cat come in?'

'Well, I don't usually let her in when I'm with a client because she can be a distraction.'

'Do you think you could make an exception?'

Patrick – who was all for going with the flow – brought the cat in. 'Judy, this is Maisie.'

'Can I just sit here and stroke her? Can I just not talk for a while? Would you mind?'

So Maisie sat in Judy's lap and was stroked in pure silence for forty-five minutes. Patrick sat perfectly still, quiet yet present. He wouldn't charge her for that session, although it was one of the best she'd ever had.

Judy stayed in town for another week. Although Barbara hadn't stopped crying completely, she wasn't doing so quite as much, and she'd started eating again – a limited diet of nursery food: soft-boiled eggs, quarter-triangle sandwiches on white bread, cheese on toast. Judy had repainted the spare room one afternoon with Gina's help, and all but a few select reminders of Ray had now been removed from the house. Judy had been careful to ensure that Barbara wouldn't come across his gloves in the hall drawers or spectacles that were a good two prescriptions ago. The coat stand looked emaciated, but at least it contained no surprises, no ghosts. Auntie Jo had promised to visit most days – the sisters had become closer now they were both widows, bonded by loss. Jo had confided in Judy that she wished she could reassure her sister that the moments of panic would subside and would eventually stop altogether. She wished she could make her believe that she would, one day, laugh again, and that she might even dance again.

Judy had tried to arrange to see Paul before she left, but he'd been elusive and she sensed she was being edged out of his inner circle. Since they'd last met, most of her texts to him had received no reply. He'd attended the funeral alone but had stayed close to Oliver. She hadn't had a chance to speak to either of them on the day.

Before she left, she cooked batches of food that she divided into the smallest containers she could find, and labelled them before placing them in her mum's freezer.

'I might as well throw some of this stuff out,' said Barbara, pulling out pepperoni pizzas and quarter-pounder burgers. 'I won't eat it.'

By early evening, the freezer had been emptied, cleaned and restocked with a couple of dozen mismatched containers of spaghetti Bolognese, Irish stew and cottage pie. Only a bag of peas and a tub of vanilla ice cream survived the cull.

Later that evening, while Barbara was in the bath, Judy took down the sympathy cards and found some old ribbon to tie them together, then put them in a drawer containing paperwork and old passports. She flicked through a blue one, even though she knew what she would see. There was her dad, in his prime, ready to take on the delights of Paris and Rome. He was wearing a very smart suit and tie and had clearly just had a haircut. She could imagine what he'd smelt like in that photo booth. What was the name of the stuff in the red and

269

white tin that he put on his hair? It hit her that she had forgotten a lot already, and there was stuff that she didn't know and now never would. She knew the basics and mentally recited them to embed them a little deeper: he loved to waltz, his favourite song had been 'Strangers In The Night', his secret crush was Debbie Harry (but he always claimed it was Katharine Hepburn if anyone asked), he could not be trusted around the purple hazelnut chocolates in a Quality Street tin, and he had drunk about 50 per cent more than he claimed to. She knew his waist and chest measurements and could spot if any glove would have fitted him or not. He'd liked sweaters made from merino wool, although he didn't know it was called 'merino wool', and had had a passionate hatred of white collars on coloured shirts. He had voted Labour all his life, even when they disappointed him, and had paid the extra political contribution of his union dues. She could make a good guess at other things, like his favourite meal and his favourite author, but she didn't know which toothpaste he'd preferred or which of his neighbours he'd have least liked to be stuck in a lift with. All that had gone with him. It wasn't stuff she could ask Mum or Rob or Auntie Jo, either. She thought of him lying on his back in his best suit, his head on a needless pillow, trapped in the dark. And then the phone rang.

'I just wanted to let you know I'm not avoiding you. Rob said you're going back tomorrow.'

It was Paul.

'I was just thinking about Dad. I don't know what tooth-paste …' She started to cry.

270

'Shall I come over?'

'No. No. Stay there.'

'You come here, then.'

There's barely a buried individual whose lowering into the ground hasn't sparked the kind of sex that's motivated by coming face to face with one's own mortality. There's always at least one person at any given funeral who is planning their next sexual encounter, often with someone sitting in a different pew. It's one of those rare situations where the attractiveness of the back of someone's head or a fetching hat could result in a very hot date and possibly marriage. This kind of rash behaviour shouldn't be confused with comfort sex. Comfort sex is all about the warmth, physical contact and being held afterwards. Sex to avoid death is a different matter altogether. It's all about the sex, and being held afterwards is merely foreplay for the next round. Sex to avoid death may well result in a baby being born nine months later – a little bit of immortality for the parties concerned – but it's not always the case. Same-sex couples and those for whom conceiving would be beyond the realms of possibility also go for it.

'Come in,' said Paul, as he hugged his bereaved friend on the doorstep.

They'd been talking for an hour before Paul kissed her. It was a nuzzling and tender kiss that lied about where it was going later that night. No comfort was going to come of this. Before she considered Fabiana, Judy thought about a burlesque show she'd seen in the summer, and incorporated some of the moves she'd had the best feedback on so far. She actually growled at one point, and bit him twice, once in genuine passion and again when she remembered Fabiana. And then her brain kicked in, showering the scene with bullets of guilt and inferiority.

'I can't.'

'Come on. You can. Don't stop.'

'I can't.'

'Jude.' He held her face. 'Jude. It's us.'

And she rolled back towards him for end-of-the-world, nothing-else-matters, fuck-the-consequences sex. It was utterly, utterly glorious. The woman in the next flat conceived later that night. There were two standing ovations in the Jazz Bar, 250 miles north.

Death is not the end.

Not for those who are left behind.

CHAPTER 37

'W$_{\text{E ARE GATHERED HERE}}$ today to witness the marriage of Paul and Fabiana.'

Some months had passed.

'Judy, can you just pop my bag under the pew, please?' Barbara was a vision in blush today, groomed and poised. After seeing the wardrobe half empty, she'd finished the job and sent most of her old clothes the way of Ray's. Then, on the advice of *Woman and Home*, she had spent an entire day with a personal shopper (whose services were free – who knew?) and had been delighted to see herself through the eyes of a kind and hopeful stranger. She was now a size twelve, not a sixteen – good Lord! – and had been prescribed bigger cups and smaller straps on her bras.

As Judy bent over to pick up her mother's bag, Oliver was reminded of his ex-wife's perfect skin. Isabella, who was no fool, stroked his thigh and reminded him of how she had woken him earlier that morning.

Alberto Ferreira made a beeline for Barbara at the reception, and danced with her all evening. He sang along beautifully in Portuguese to some of the songs, but he couldn't persuade her to step out for some air on the balcony, despite promising her all the verses of 'Bésame Mucho'. Judy bobbed from table to table and eventually settled with Gina and George, who seemed to be in the middle of an argument.

The groom came over.

'So, Ms Taylor, you made it. How very lovely to have your presence here at my humble wedding with its three hundred guests, half of whom speak little or no English. How are you?'

'I'm fine, Mr Roberts. And may I congratulate you on your nuptials and your choice of beautiful wife. May you live long and happy lives and produce many offspring.'

'We are working on that very thing, but the judicious choice of foundation garments means that nobody will suspect a thing on this, our special day.'

'Oh!'

'Don't breathe a word.'

'No. No, I won't. Well, congratulations.'

'Thanks. How are you? Come here, give us a kiss. We're allowed – it's my wedding day.'

They pecked each other's cheeks. A frisson.

'I'm fine. Just finalizing the details, then I'll be the proud owner of the tiniest coffee shop you could ever imagine.'

'Great. That's great.'

'Excellent coffee. You should come and try it with your wife.'

'I will,' he lied.

'Very interesting customers.'

'I'd like to think I could bring the tone down.'

'There's a man who composes music based on people's DNA – they pay thousands for it.'

'Did I tell you about the student who asked me if I'd wet her painting with my saliva, to show my influence in her work?'

'Aren't people just fascinating? What's not to love? Anyway, it's only a couple of hundred miles up the road. Less than three hours on the train. I'll even throw in free muffins as long as it's not August.'

'I'll consult my diary.'

Fabiana had spotted the loaded body language behind the friendly cheek pecks, and slinked over to reclaim her husband. 'Paul, you must come and speak to my aunt and uncle before they go to bed.' Her accent made even the most innocent invitation seem like a siren call.

And so he was led away. Fabiana clearly had no wish to speak to the woman who had bought them a damn fine coffee maker as a wedding present.

Barbara and her daughter locked eyes across the room and gravitated towards each other.

'Are you ready for home, Mum?'

'I am. My feet are killing me. Alberto's danced me around this hall as though I were a woman half my age.'

Barbara was going to be OK.

'Have you spoken to Rob and Min?'

'Yes, we had a nice chat,' lied Judy. It was only a white lie because, on the surface, to anyone listening in, it *had* been a nice chat. But it was the kind of chat that had an undercurrent rumbling beneath it, threatening to break through any weak spots in the veneer.

'That's nice. They both look exhausted. Charlie's not sleeping well, you know. They're up half the night.'

' Yes. They said.'

They exited smoothly, the luxury afforded peripheral guests.

Paul and Fabiana flew out to Brazil a couple of months after their wedding. Paul taught until the end of term, and used the money from the sale of his and Jen's flat to set up a small football coaching school in Fabiana's home town. He would speak two languages fluently in a few years' time. Fabiana gave birth to twin boys and, a year later, a daughter. The couple would live to see their grandson play football for his country. Ahead of them lay more than half a century of happiness and good health, and they would die as peacefully as one can, within a fortnight of each other.

The man who arranged the finance for Judy's coffee shop was the kind of man Ray and Barbara had hoped she would bring home one day. Even his name sounded reliable: John. It was an honest name that didn't rely on any additional syllables to hold it up. He was taller than Judy by two inches, smartly dressed during the week and smart-casual at weekends. He only ever wore shorts on holiday, and they were navy cotton with no logo. He had no tattoos and, it surely goes without saying, no piercings. He didn't have a degree because he had wanted to 'get out there and earn' as a bright teenager but he was a fair intellectual sparring partner for any graduate of a middling university. He visited his parents frequently enough to show them he cared but not enough to irritate any future partner. He owned a two-bedroom flat in Edinburgh (mortgage paid off), had shares in a fish-canning factory in Norway and owned a holiday villa (with pool) in Marbella.

He had tried to woo Judy in several stages, at first over profit-and-loss figures and then over endless coffees. She had been surprised that setting up the finance on the coffee shop had necessitated so many face-to-face meetings but had put it down to the jittery financial climate. When he moved in for a kiss after she'd locked up one night, she had laughed, which was unforgivable, but the shock, combined with the exhaustion of working seven days a week for three months, had worn away her social skills to the point at which they were only evident to paying customers and her cherished staff.

'I'm sorry.' He was mortified and completely thrown by the laugh. He had been convinced that he'd detected signals.

'I'm sorry, John. I'm just a bit surprised and—'

'No, please. I'll leave you in peace.'

He started to fumble as he hurriedly gathered his things together. His pen rolled off the desk and he bumped heads with

Judy as they both went to retrieve it. It was truly an awkward moment. In the back of his mind, he had thought it might be the kind of moment one might tell one's grandchildren about in the future – 'We bumped heads, and that was where it all started.' He thought of Ryan O'Neal and Barbra Streisand in *What's Up, Doc?*. The image of Judy lying on a piano covered with a white cloth was almost too much for him to bear.

'I hope I've not upset you, Judy, it's just that I find you very attractive, and I—'

Judy jumped in to save him from more embarrassment. 'John, please, can we just … I'm very flattered and I think you're a lovely guy, but I'm just not looking for anyone right now. I'm trying to get the business off the ground and—' *Jesus, this is the last thing I need!*

He'd heard brush-offs like that all his life; most hadn't been as kind. She was out of his league, of course she was.

'No, please. It's all my fault, Judy. I'll go now, and leave you in peace, as I said, and I'll be in touch.'

Judy unlocked the door so that he could back out of it rather than into it. There'd been enough slapstick for one evening.

That night, as she climbed into bed, she let out a laugh. She had never been wooed by anyone with dreadlocks, tattoos, a criminal record or a patchy work ethic. Her fate seemed to be that she would always be pursued by nice men who wanted a nice girl with all the trimmings.

Later that week, Judy hammered up the story for Lily's delight, tacking a slapstick ending on to it for a finale. Lily laughed and rocked in her chair, and Judy saw the girl she had once been, the girl Joe had fallen in love with sixty years ago.

'That poor man,' laughed Lily.

'Have you seen this bruise on my head?'

'Who the hell says, "I find you very attractive", for God's sake?' She clutched her sides and laughed until she ran out of breath.

'I mean, he's a lovely man, but really …'

'Oh, you've scarred him for life, so you have!' More laughter.

It occurred to Judy that they were laughing, essentially, at the parlous state of her love life, but somehow it felt OK. She felt no compunction to fix it. She rather liked the unpredictability of it all, for now.

As Judy ran home, she thought of Lily left in the silence.

The beat-beat-beat of her feet carried her into the wide open mouth of the deepest, blackest mine and she started to cry. She cried for Lily, for Oliver, for her dad and mum, for Jen, for Paul, for home. The gut-wrenching sobs were mainly for herself, for the life she had left behind and the one she had chosen. Her chosen life seemed to be punctuated by these snot-filled, uncontrollable moments.

She was no longer one of those women who would perch on the sidelines, meting out their bodily fluids in small fortnightly colds, acceptable sex and little monthly weeps, dabbing at their eyes with their index fingers wrapped in sleeves, over soap-opera weddings and fluctuating hormones, avoiding the wet patch, sniffling and sneezing and being blessed and *gesundheit*ed by colleagues. Her life had once been filled with manageable, bearable incremental stuff. There had been no white-knuckle plunges, death howls or orgasms that resonated across stars and galaxies.

Tomorrow, she would wake to the wolf-whistle of a starling.

ACKNOWLEDGEMENTS

I AM ETERNALLY INDEBTED to everyone at Constable & Robinson and United Agents. Thank you to my editor, Victoria Hughes-Williams; to Jessica Craig for seeing potential in my draft manuscript; to my agent, Anna Webber, for her expertise, humour, guidance and faith; and to Clive Hebard and Saskia Angenent.

Thank you to Michèle Mendelssohn for reading every word and illuminating the journey in so many ways; to Anne Vial for seeing promise in the first few pages and for her invaluable support since; to Hazel Orme for her eagle eye and light touch; to Ali Bowden, Anna Burkey and Peggy Hughes from Edinburgh UNESCO City of Literature for exciting opportunities and kind words.

My love and gratitude to dear friends: to Dee Bingham for always staying as close to me in the dark as she has in the light and for being such an inspiration; to Kenris MacLeod for sharing in the excitement; and to dazzlingly talented writer friends, Marta Rainer and Angela Peterson Newton.

Thank you to Lisa Vickers, Viv(tastic) Monaghan, Natalie Henry, Colin and Kirsten Steele, Jasmine and Jim Bellinger, Fiona Paterson, Charlie Hides, Kath Forshaw, Dee Atkinson, Stephan Matthiesen, Bill Kyle, Shakti, Laura Sydonie and the numerous friends, students and colleagues who have provided kind words of encouragement.

Huge thanks to those who gave generously of their time and skills: to multi-talented Jane Steger-Lewis for her work and good grace; to Richard Kenyon for so much, including reading the manuscript from cover to cover and keeping it safe from crayons and bananas; and to John Elcock and his team for doing such an excellent job on www.angela-jackson.com.

Special thanks to Mr Keith Douglas for his kindness, gentle guidance and for giving me words and books in which to take refuge.

Thank you to Edinburgh International Book Festival for making my heart beat faster every August; to Bill Evans, Fred Hersch, Billy Strayhorn, Brian Kellock, Thelonius Monk, Miles Davis, Chet Baker, Colin Steele, Gina Rae & Sandy Wright, Roddy Frame, Martin Stephenson, Ben Watt and Tracey Thorn for soundtracking my writing, especially in the wee small hours; to the magical city of Edinburgh for inspiring me and the north of England for its rain, bricks, cobbles and beautiful flat vowels.